ONLY THE DEAD

VIDAR SUNDSTØL

Translated by TIINA NUNNALLY

MINNESOTA TRILOGY 2

University of Minnesota Press
Minneapolis

This translation has been published with the financial support of NORLA (Norwegian Literature Abroad, Fiction and Nonfiction).

Published by the University of Minnesota Press
111 Third Avenue South, Suite 290
Minneapolis, MN 55401–2520
http://www.upress.umn.edu

LIBRARY OF CONGRESS CATALOGING-IN-PUBLICATION DATA
Sundstøl, Vidar. [De Døde. English]
Only the dead / Vidar Sundstøl ; translated by Tiina Nunnally.
(Minnesota Trilogy ; 2)
ISBN 978-0-8166-8942-2 (hc)
1. Brothers—Fiction. 2. Tourists—Crimes against—Fiction. 3. Minnesota—Fiction. 4. Family secrets—Fiction. I. Nunnally, Tiina, 1952– translator. II. Title.
PT8952.29.U53D6413 2014
839.82'38—dc23
2014014122

Printed in the United States of America on acid-free paper

The University of Minnesota is an equal-opportunity educator and employer.

20 19 18 17 16 15 14   10 9 8 7 6 5 4 3 2 1

1

HIS CELL PHONE began silently vibrating in his pants pocket. Lance Hansen cautiously took it out and checked the display, but the number was not one he recognized. Just as cautiously he put the phone back. Then he again gripped his rifle with both hands.

It was sprinkling a bit, making a few rippling rings on the surface of the water. His cell was still vibrating. He wondered who could be calling him. At that moment he saw a buck emerge from the woods across the lake. It paused, its body erect and alert. A drop of water was forming at the tip of Lance's nose, but he didn't want to risk wiping it off. The slightest movement might give him away. He concentrated on standing still, not even shifting his gaze. Through the light rain coming down over the lake, the deer looked like part of the landscape. Someone who was not observant would have had a very hard time noticing that it was standing there at all.

The deer turned its head to look back toward the woods. Quickly and silently Lance raised his rifle, took aim, and found the deer in his scope. All of a sudden it was very close. He could see how the damp was making the rough hairs of the outer coat stick together in patterns of darker stripes, and steam was rising from the animal's warm body. But this was not a large buck, and when it again turned its head, he saw that its antlers were small and asymmetrical.

As soon as he lowered his rifle, the deer froze. Then it disappeared, bounding away with long, springy strides. The last he saw of it was the raised white tail.

His cell phone had stopped vibrating. He wiped the drop from his nose. The branches of the tall maple trees down by the mouth of the creek were bare. Here and there a solitary yellow leaf still clung to a birch twig. The puddles on the boggy ground had thick layers of rotting leaves on the bottom. Twice before he had brought down a deer at Copper Pond, as the small lake was called. Both times he had stood partially hidden behind the very same shaggy fir tree. From here he had a clear shot across the water, with no obstructing bushes or trees. It was approximately a hundred yards to the spot where the deer usually came out of the woods.

He glanced at his watch. They would have to stop soon if they were going to get back to their cars before dark. Somewhere in the woods over there, his brother, Andy, was on his way toward the lake. He was supposed to call before he showed up. That was how they made sure that the person doing the driving didn't end up in the line of fire. As long as the driver hadn't called, the poster was free to shoot at any deer that appeared. As soon as the driver called to say he was approaching, all shooting was banned. That was also why they couldn't take calls from anyone else. If they did, they risked getting a busy signal when they tried to phone each other. This was the new system they'd improvised after Lance, much to his surprise, had discovered earlier in the morning that the walkie-talkies they always used were not in their usual place in the garage. There was no sign of a break-in, and it had been a long time since he'd last checked their communications equipment, so he decided he must have moved them himself and then forgotten about it. At any rate, there had been no time to get hold of new walkie-talkies.

Again he focused his attention on the edge of the woods across the lake. He studied one small patch at a time before moving his gaze to another area. The overriding grays and browns of the November landscape made it difficult to catch sight of a deer. It was a matter of keeping out extraneous thoughts and simply scanning his surroundings, on the lookout for the arch of a neck or the sway of a back among all the other organic shapes in the woods.

After a moment he glanced at his watch again, but only ten minutes had passed. Since dusk would settle in soon, he decided he'd better try calling his brother.

When the phone had rung five or six times, Lance realized that he wasn't going to get an answer. Even so, he let it keep ringing. Presumably Andy was closing in on a deer. The driver usually walked with the wind at his back in order to scare the animals forward toward the hunter waiting on post, but today there was no wind. The light rain was falling straight down. Under these circumstances it was possible to sneak up on a deer, and his brother was an expert at doing just that. He could move so quietly that not even a deer could hear him.

After Lance had stood there for another five minutes without hearing anything from his brother, he decided to call it a day. He might as well go back to the cars and wait there. That was the usual procedure if they couldn't find each other.

He slung the strap of his rifle over his shoulder and began heading toward the south end of the lake, where the creek ran out of it. Crossing the boggy ground took some effort. He was a heavy man, and for every step he took, he had to drag his feet up from the gurgling muck. When he reached the mouth of the creek, he sat down on a rock. He sat there in the rain, breathing hard. Above him the naked gray branches of the maple trees stretched toward the rainy sky. The drops were falling faster now, a pattering cold rain. He noticed that steam was rising off him, just as it had from the body of the deer he'd taken aim at only a short time ago.

Then he got to his feet and started walking along the creek, which passed through a culvert beneath the road, right near their parked cars. It shouldn't take more than ten minutes for him to get there. Spruce trees stood close together on either side, creating a semidarkness filled with the sound of running water. At one spot he had to descend a steep, muddy slope near a little waterfall. The ground was slippery, and he slid rather than clambered down to the pool at the base of the waterfall. There he crouched down next to the creek and rinsed off his mud-covered hands. The temperature had dropped so low that he didn't notice any significant difference when he stuck his hands in the water. As he stood up, he saw something move in the woods, maybe twenty yards away. Only for a second, a glimpse of something dark. Automatically he reached for his rifle, which he'd leaned against a tree trunk, but then stopped himself; he thought it might have been a person, someone who had quickly retreated. Lance was still standing there, bending forward, with his arm stretched out and his hand ready to pick up the rifle. He listened intently but it was utterly quiet, except for the raindrops striking his jacket and the churning sound of the little waterfall.

His phone began vibrating again. Another number he didn't recognize. When it stopped ringing, he checked the previous call and saw that it was the same number both times. Someone was clearly trying to get hold of him, but it wasn't his brother.

The crackling sound of maple leaves under his boots told him the temperature must be around freezing. The rain might even turn to snow during the night. He made a few abrupt stops so he could stand still and listen. But why would anyone be following him?

He reached the gravel road. There stood his brother's white Chevy Blazer with the red door on the right-hand side and his own black Jeep Cherokee. They had parked at the end of a long, straight stretch of road. He took the magazine out of his rifle and removed the cartridge from the chamber. Then he placed the rifle inside his Jeep, got in, and turned on the engine.

A CD of the program *Car Talk* was in the stereo. The two hosts, who were brothers, had a woman from Washington, D.C., on the line. They were discussing an ethical question that had something to do with a borrowed car and a fine. He didn't catch all the details. Finally they said she was just going to have to pay up. Either that, or get herself a gun. When she told them she already had a gun, one of the hosts said, in that case, why was she bothering to call them?

After trying to phone his brother one more time without getting an answer, Lance pulled up his hood and stepped back out into the cold rain, going over to the Chevy. Both doors were locked, as they should be. There was a copy of *Guns & Ammo* on the passenger seat. In the back he could see work clothes, tools, oil cans, several pairs of logger boots, a hard hat, and other types of gear for work. Everything looked perfectly normal, except for the fact that his brother hadn't arrived. And the fact that he wasn't picking up his phone.

A twig snapped. Lance turned around, prepared to see Andy emerging from the woods, but that didn't happen. The wall of spruce trees stood motionless before him.

5

"Hello?" he said.

Not a sound from the forest.

"Hello?" he ventured again, louder this time, but no one replied.

He picked up a rock and threw it at the trees, then stood still and listened, but he heard only the raindrops landing on his hood. For a few more seconds he stood there, staring into the darkness between the trees. Then he turned on his heel and went back to his Jeep. He knew what it was he'd just heard. The unmistakable sound of a dry twig snapping under the weight of a body. Could it have been something other than a person? Maybe a moose or a deer? Doubtful in such a dense part of the woods.

He was feeling a little foolish, but he didn't want to take any chances, so he backed a good distance down the road before he parked again. Someone had been over by the creek too. A brief glimpse, a movement, as if someone had retreated so as not to be seen.

The forest was just as dense and dark here as where he'd stood before. It was raining harder now. The Chevy had become a blurry, gray patch at the end of the long flat clearing. Soon there would be no point in continuing to wait for his brother. For a moment Lance was tempted to switch off his phone and just sit there. Not try to contact anyone. Or organize a search party. Just sit there on this gravel road deep inside the forest as evening turned into night, and let somebody else take responsibility.

He jumped when he heard a knock on the passenger-side window of the Jeep. Outside he saw his brother's face pressed close to the glass.

"DID YOU LOSE YOUR PHONE?" he asked as soon as Andy opened the Jeep door.

"No."

"I've been trying to call you."

Andy dug his cell out of his pocket and looked at it. "Out of juice," he said in surprise. "I must have forgotten to charge it."

The whole car smelled of his brother. His sweat mixed with rain. His thin hair hanging straight down, cut as if a bowl had been placed on his head. His clothes. His breath. Lance had known that smell all his life.

"So, did you see any deer?"

"One," said Lance.

"A buck?"

"Yeah."

"Too small?"

"Yeah."

Andy's face looked drawn and worn out. Lance had noticed this earlier in the day too. He must not be sleeping well lately, he thought.

"Where'd you come from?" he asked his brother.

"Copper Pond, as we agreed, but you weren't there."

"Why didn't you phone me?"

"My cell was dead."

"But you didn't notice that until now."

"I tried . . ."

"But what?"

"My cell wasn't working," Andy repeated.

"Then why did you look so surprised right now?"

Something didn't add up. There was something he needed to find out.

"Lance . . ." said Andy with a resigned sigh. He fidgeted with his rifle, which he'd placed between his legs, with the butt stock on the floor and the barrel propped against his shoulder.

"What?" said Lance, sounding impatient and annoyed.

Andy bit his lip, which was something he always did whenever he was feeling nervous.

"You know that break-in at the cabin this summer?" he said.

The change of subject was so blatant that Lance could hardly believe his ears.

"When I got there, I saw that the rock I usually keep the spare key under was lying on the ground."

Lance thought about how he'd initially searched for the key, and then used the rock to break a window. He'd been looking for answers, fueled by a growing suspicion regarding his brother and the murder near Baraga's Cross.

"So?" he said now. "What about it?"

"Somebody must have been looking for the key, but you told me you thought some kids had broken in. They wouldn't know where I hid the key."

"Right. That was me, when I discovered the break-in. I thought the key might be in the usual place."

The only thing of interest Lance had found in the cabin was a copy of the music magazine *Darkside,* and the only one who could have possibly brought it there was Andy's seventeen-year-old daughter, Chrissy. Since it was the latest issue, she must have been at the cabin sometime during the three weeks before the murder. She might even have been there on the night the man was killed. According to Andy's wife, Tammy, father and daughter had returned home together on the day after the murder. Andy claimed to have gone to the cabin to do some fishing, while Chrissy had spent the night with a girlfriend in Duluth. At least that was how Tammy had described her family's movements during that twenty-four-hour period.

"Why would you go looking for the key after you discovered someone broke in?" asked Andy.

"What exactly are you trying to say?"

"It just puzzles me. That's all."

Lance stared straight ahead without saying anything. He could no longer see the Chevy.

"Well, whatever." Andy pulled up his hood. "It's getting late."

"Hmm," muttered Lance.

"What about tomorrow?" Andy opened the car door.

"I suppose we should . . ."

"Yes, we should. I was thinking maybe . . . Cross River. Above the road."

"Why there?" asked Lance.

"A big buck has been roaming around up there all summer."

"I never heard about that."

Andy got out of the car. "Shall we say eight o'clock in the parking lot near the bridge?" He had one hand on the door, ready to close it. In his other hand he held the rifle.

"Okay," said Lance. "Eight o'clock at Cross River."

His brother shut the door without saying good-bye. Lance tried to watch him as he headed for his own vehicle, but he was instantly swallowed up by the dark.

THE WET ASPHALT gleamed in the light from the North Shore Market in Tofte. A few cars drove past on Highway 61. On the other side of the road was the Coho Café, closed now for the winter, and beyond it nothing but impenetrable darkness. Henry was standing behind the counter in the grocery store, wearing glasses with thick lenses and one of his usual flannel shirts. His scalp was clearly visible through the sparse strands of his straw-colored hair.

Lance Hansen had walked down all the aisles without

putting a single item in his shopping basket. Now he was back where he'd started, at the front counter. He was cold and wet and in need of a hot meal.

"Been out hunting?" asked Henry.

"Yep."

"Get anything?"

"Nope."

He pretended that he'd suddenly remembered something and made another round of the aisles. At the meat counter at the very back of the store he saw only a couple of bratwursts and some roast beef that had gone gray after a long day. For a moment he stopped to stare at the packages of Land O'Lakes butter and the bottles of milk lined up behind the glass doors in the cooler. Not that he needed milk or butter, but he'd always liked that logo showing the beautiful Indian maiden in front of a dazzling blue lake.

He heard the front door open as someone came into the store. A woman's voice replied to something Henry said. Lance went over to the shelves of snacks and put a bag of Old Dutch potato chips in his basket. Without further hesitation he went over to the canned foods section and grabbed the first one he saw. Beefaroni was just as good as anything else.

On his way back to the counter, he practically ran right into Becky Tofte.

"Hey, Lance!" she exclaimed, putting her hand on his arm, as she usually did. "Long time no see."

"Uh-huh."

She was holding a box of Betty Crocker brownie mix in her other hand as she looked at him.

"Have you been out in the woods?"

"Deer hunting."

Outside a lumber truck and trailer drove by. The vibration from the weight of the vehicle and the double load of lumber started things clattering somewhere in the store.

"So how's it going?" asked Becky when the noise faded.

"Things are good."

He noticed that she had pursed her lips, as if trying to make up her mind about something.

"You look . . . ," she began, but then stopped.

Lance glanced away.

"Already November," she said. "It'll soon be Thanksgiving again."

"Uh-huh."

"We haven't seen much of you lately. At the station, I mean."

"There's been a lot going on out in the field."

"Really?"

"Yeah."

He couldn't decide where to look. Becky gave the Betty Crocker box a little shake. "Well, I'd better see about getting home to make these," she said. Then she touched his arm again, turned on her heel, and left the store.

Lance stayed where he was among the aisles, waiting until he heard Becky start up her car and drive off. Only then did he go over to the counter and set down his shopping basket. As he stood there, watching nearsighted Henry ring up his purchases on the old-fashioned cash register, he caught sight of the heart-shaped Dove chocolates in the candy rack. Out of habit, he grabbed a handful.

HE WAS JOLTED AWAKE by a loud bang. It took him a couple of seconds to figure out where it had come from. A car was on fire on TV. He found the remote control and turned down the sound. His plate with the fork and the congealed Beefaroni was still sitting on the table. And next to it was an empty beer bottle. Mesabi Red. He tried to remember if he'd been dreaming about something, but his mind was blank, as usual.

He hadn't had a dream in more than seven years now. In his last dream he had been climbing down some steep mountain slopes. Below him lay a huge body of water that he recognized as Lake Superior. It was light enough for him to see where he placed his feet, and he was breathing and moving as easily as he did on land. On closer reflection, he wasn't really sure if that was how the dream started or not. The beginning might have been different, more chaotic, something he could no longer recall. Something that was impossible to put into words.

As he remembered the dream, it began with him halfway down a mountainside, in the process of making his way farther down. And there weren't just mountains down there. He also saw a muddy plain with several old trees, their trunks smooth and hard, their branches sticking out in all directions. At last he stood below on the uneven, icy lake bottom, where it was as bright as the day above. No, it was a more bluish light. Spreading out around him was a landscape of icebergs, shimmering blue. He knew at once that he was at the deepest spot in the lake. No one had ever seen this before, nor would anyone ever see it again. Beauty like this existed nowhere else but here. The cold from the icebergs began eating into his body. Very fast. He was turning rigid, his marrow freezing, his bones filling up with ice. Soon he wouldn't be able to move. That was when he awoke, drenched with sweat.

He got up from the sofa and cleared the table, carrying everything out to the kitchen. It was already eight. He'd been asleep for almost an hour. From the living room he could hear the weather report for Minnesota. He rushed back to the sofa and turned up the sound on the TV, but the report was almost over. The only thing he heard was something about "difficult driving conditions in the northeast." It wouldn't have bothered him if the driving conditions got so bad that they'd have to cancel their hunting expedition. He regretted not shooting that deer today; if he had, that would have been the end of it. A whole year until the next hunting season. Instead, he was going to have to spend tomorrow with Andy. He had the distinct feeling his brother knew who was behind the break-in at his cabin. But did he also know why? Did he know that Lance knew?

His cell rang. He picked it up from the coffee table and saw that it was the same number as earlier in the day. This time he answered.

"Lance Hansen."

"Ah, there you are," he heard his former father-in-law say.

"Willy?"

"Yes."

"Where are you calling from?"

"Here."

"Did you borrow a phone from somebody?"

"No. Mary bought me a . . . one of those . . ."

"Cell phones? Did Mary buy you a cell?"

"Yes. She's afraid I'll drown."

"What?"

"She says this is safer. I don't know . . . I guess she thinks I can use it to float if I fall into the lake."

"I saw that you tried to call me earlier today."

"Yes."

"I was out deer hunting."

"Oh, really? Did you shoot any deer?"

"No. I *could* have shot one, but I let it go."

"Oh?"

"Yeah. It was too small."

Lance had talked to Willy Dupree on only one occasion in the past three years. That was four months ago. He'd paid a visit to the elderly Ojibwe to ask him about an old photograph.

"Was there something special you wanted to talk to me about?" he asked now.

The old man muttered something.

"What?" said Lance.

"There's something I need to tell you," said Willy, speaking a little louder.

"Okay . . ."

"But you have to come here . . . tonight."

"It takes me an hour and a half to drive out to Grand Portage. Couldn't you tell me now?"

"On the phone?"

"Uh-huh."

"No."

"Why not?"

"No."

"I don't really know if I can . . ."

"You have to."

2

March 1892

Fat fish that I could cook and eat and drink the broth from afterward. It makes me dizzy just thinking about it. But it's impossible to catch the fish in the lake. First I need to get me a boat. Then I can set out some nets and bring them up full of fish. The water is gurgling underneath, at the edge of the ice. The moon is shining. I'm sitting on the snowshoes that are tied to the back of my knapsack, leaning back against a big black rock that's capped with snow.

I saw it from far away. There's something about rocks standing all alone like that. Almost as if they were houses. As if people lived here. But there's no one around. I hack off a piece of the icy crust of snow and stuff it in my mouth. Suck on it. I brought along only the few things I had room for. Some clothes, a little food, my Bible, and an ax. I bought the ax in town. I thought it best to have my own ax if I'm going to look for work in the woods. So I went with Mr. Dahl to a shop that sold all kinds of axes. But I didn't like the town. No, I definitely did not. And then there's the language. I can hardly understand anything. Only a few words: yes, no, ticket, dollar, food, train, room, water. And moon. Hard to believe it's the same moon as back home.

I'd better stand up now and get moving. Can't stay sitting here in this cold. There's nothing left of the food Mrs. Dahl gave me to take along. I haven't eaten since . . . I don't know how long. No food left in my bag, just some clothes and the ax and my Bible. Hard to believe it was only a year ago I was confirmed. "I the Lord thy God am a jealous God, visiting the iniquity of the fathers upon the children unto the third and fourth generation of them that hate me; And shewing mercy unto thousands of them that love me, and keep my commandments."

I got up and have started walking again. In some places the ice stretches so far that I can barely see the water way off in the distance. In other places it's such a narrow strip that I can hear a gurgling under the edge. The water is completely black, with moonlight shining on it. The snow is smooth and slippery and I think there must be rocks underneath. Smooth rocks all along this huge lake. In the summertime it must get so hot that you could burn your hand if you touched them.

The fish are supposedly so big they almost look human. That's what I've heard. Fish as big as grown men. I fought with one of them. Or was that something I dreamed? Am I asleep? No, I'm walking along the lake with my eyes open. Or am I asleep standing up, dreaming that my eyes are open? I tell myself that this is a dream. And then I open my eyes. I can hardly believe what I see. Because I'm still sitting on the rock. I haven't budged. And I'm so cold. I was dreaming about fish as big as grown men and that I was fighting with one of those fish in the shallow water. But it's deadly dangerous to fall asleep in cold weather like this. I haul myself up. My legs are aching with cold. To make sure I'm not asleep, I blink my eyes again and again. This better not be a dream.

THE RAIN WAS JUST A LIGHT DRIZZLE, almost like dew hitting the windshield. The wipers were set at the slowest speed. Occasionally the glow from the headlights swept over a dark wall of spruce trees. Lance was thinking about Andy knocking on the window on the passenger side of the Jeep and peering through the glass. He should have come out of the woods on the other side of the road if he was coming from Copper Pond, the way he'd claimed. And if so, wouldn't he have knocked on the window on the driver's side, where Lance was sitting? No matter what, he must have reached the road from somewhere behind the Jeep; otherwise Lance would have seen his brother walking toward him. But he hadn't noticed anything until Andy knocked on the window. At that point he'd already moved the Jeep about a hundred yards. It seemed unlikely his brother would have entered the road so far away from where they had parked. He would have followed the creek from Copper Pond just as Lance had done, which meant Lance would have seen him coming. Had Andy even been at Copper Pond?

And what about the communications equipment? The walkie-talkies were always kept on a shelf near the ceiling in the garage, but this morning they were missing. He thought about the fact that Andy hadn't answered his phone. His explanation had been anything but convincing.

At that moment, out of the corner of his eye, Lance noticed something moving. He heard two thuds as something struck the car. It all happened so fast he didn't even have time to brake. He stopped, put the car in reverse, and began to back up. Luckily it was a long, straight stretch of road with no traffic right now. After about a hundred yards he parked on the shoulder and put on his emergency lights. Only then did he start to think about what sort of animal he might have hit. All he'd seen was something moving fast on the road in front of his car. Maybe a badger or a hare. Not a big animal, at any rate.

He got out the flashlight that he always kept on the floor of the Jeep and opened the door. The cold, raw air smelled of the forest. Even though he was sure it had to be some small animal, he felt hesitant about where he set his feet on the ground in the dark. Then he pulled himself together. He shined the flashlight around but didn't see anything out of the ordinary. He aimed the light at the ditch, but saw only dirt and stones. After walking a short way along the shoulder in both directions, he gave up and went back to his vehicle. He was just about to get in when he heard a hissing sound close by. Again he aimed the flashlight at the asphalt and along the ditch but didn't see anything. But the hissing didn't stop. Finally he squatted down and shined the light under the Jeep. Two eyes gleamed at him, and now the hissing erupted into a shrill screech. It was a big white cat lying there.

Lance got in the Jeep and backed up a few yards, then got out again. The cat was lying in the same spot on the road, apparently unable to move. He opened the tailgate, using the beam of the flashlight to look through the junk inside. A big wrench was the best thing he could find. Lance grabbed it and went over to the cat, which was staring up at him and hissing. Then he leaned down as he raised the wrench. He was so close that he could clearly see the cat's face. Its lips were drawn back, its teeth gleamed white in the glow from the flashlight. Just as he was about to bring down the wrench, the cat uttered another shriek, loud and shrill. For a moment fear seized him. Then he struck.

The wrench hit something soft. The shrieking stopped abruptly, then started up again, even louder. He struck again, but it was impossible to hold the beam steady as he slammed the wrench down, and this time it hit the asphalt. Pain shot up into his shoulder. He tossed the flashlight aside and began pounding with the heavy wrench. The feel of the soft body under the blows of the wrench made him furious. The animal offered no resistance, and yet it refused to die, continuing to howl. Then he became aware of the sound of a car approaching, and he looked up. The car came driving along the flat clearing, gradually slowing its speed. Finally it stopped right next to the Jeep, only a few yards away. A gurgling sound came from the cat as he kept on hitting it. The stranger in the other car didn't move, and Lance had the feeling he was being watched as he delivered one blow after another, faster and faster. After a moment the car drove off, and he was alone. The only sound was his own breathing, and the blows that kept on striking the cat's body in the dark.

"I DREAMED that I found a wooden figure of two people holding hands," said Willy Dupree. He was sitting there with his eyes closed, looking as if he were asleep.

"Over near the lake, after a storm. I went there as I always do, to see what might have drifted ashore this time, and that's when I caught sight of that wooden figure lying there. It wasn't much bigger than a grown man's fist. I picked it up to take a closer look. It was a tree root, or . . . it was both a root and something that someone had carved. It was both things at the same time. That's possible in dreams, you know. It was smooth, as if newly whittled or as if the bark had just been stripped off. Totally new and fresh. And as I said, it looked like two people holding hands."

Lance waited for him to go on, but the old man just sat there with his eyes closed and his hands clasped over his stomach. Had he dozed off?

"Did anything else happen?" Lance ventured.

Willy opened his eyes. "No. Then I woke up."

"And this is why I had to drive all the way out here? To hear this?"

"No. My dream reminded me of something. That's why I called you, but you didn't answer the phone. You were out hunting."

"That's right."

"Alone?"

"No, with Andy. I was on post when you called. Andy was driving."

"I thought these days everybody shot deer from platforms up in the trees."

"Not us."

"It's supposed to be much easier. That's what I've heard."

"But hunting isn't supposed to be easy."

"No, no, I guess not . . ."

"So what did you want to tell me?'

"Well, you know the spirit huts that we build over our graves?"

Lance nodded. He'd seen the small wooden structures erected in old Ojibwe cemeteries, built to cover the whole length of the grave.

"People used to put things inside that the dead person might need on the journey to the realm of the dead. Food and tobacco, for instance. Preferably something that the deceased was particularly fond of when he was alive. A special pipe, maybe, or a gun. Swamper Caribou was a great medicine man, a sort of priest, if you will. There's no doubt that he would have been given a traditional burial, but no one ever found his body. When I was young, I heard an old man talk about Swamper disappearing. He remembered when it happened, you see. He said that several other medicine men came here to Grand Portage to discuss what had happened. And since he disappeared while he was staying at the lake—he was trapping mink and otters down by Cross River—they decided to build a canoe and send it out on the water with things his spirit would need on the journey. They made a small version of an ordinary canoe. I don't remember anymore exactly what they put in it. Except for one thing, and that was Swamper Caribou's knife, which he always carried with him in this life. I think it was found inside his hunting cabin, and they thought he would need it on the other side. Finally, they sang a sacred song over the canoe before they sent it out onto the lake."

Willy Dupree slowly leaned forward to pick up his glass of water from the table. His hand was shaking badly as he raised it to his lips. He drank greedily. The old man's Adam's apple moved up and down under his slack skin. Then he set the glass on the table, his hand still shaking. Once again he leaned back in his chair, breathing hard. A trickle of water ran down his chin, but he didn't notice.

"All a man has left is a bunch of memories," he said.

"You have your grandson, Jimmy."

"That's true. We have our daily chat."

"Do you ever tell him the old stories?"

"Sometimes."

"About Swamper Caribou?"

"No."

"That's probably best. He might get scared."

"What about you, Lance?"

"What about me?"

"Does Swamper Caribou scare you?"

Lance tried to laugh, but it didn't come out right.

"Do you want to know what happened to his knife?"

Lance nodded.

"A man was putting out nets off Hat Point when he happened to see something floating in the water a short distance away. He paid it no mind, just kept setting out his nets. When he was done, the object had drifted closer, and he got curious, so he paddled over to it. And he found Swamper Caribou's little canoe, the one the other medicine men had made, although the man had never heard about that. All he thought was that the canoe was much too small to be of any use. But then he discovered the knife. And he could always use an extra knife. No matter what, he couldn't figure out what it was doing out there on the lake in a little birchbark canoe. Since it didn't seem to belong to anyone, he picked up the knife and took a closer look. The shaft was made of buckhorn, the blade so sharp that he started bleeding as soon as he touched it with his fingertip. The man decided to take the knife. When he came home, he told the whole story to his wife. She thought that if a knife appeared in that way, it must have come from the spirit world, and she told him to get rid of it. The man promised to do as she said.

"That very evening, he went over to the lake to throw the knife into the water. But just as he was about to do that, he had a sudden feeling the knife was not merely a dead object. It felt like . . . like a *friend*. And now he was supposed to throw it into the lake so it would never be found again? He couldn't make himself do it. But his wife would refuse to have it in the house if she found out he hadn't done as she asked, so on his way home the man hid the knife in a hollow tree he knew about. Every evening he would go over to that tree and take out the knife. Whenever he held it in his hand, he would get the same feeling that this was more than just a knife. He didn't know exactly what it was, but he thought it had to be magic, because it had come sailing toward him in a little canoe on the big lake, and it felt like it was alive. So he thought, just as his wife did, that the knife had some connection to the spirit world. And yet he couldn't make himself give it up.

"Soon he became so obsessed by the knife that his wife thought he was going out to the woods to be with another woman. She asked her husband if that was what he was doing, and she said she refused to accept a simple no as an answer. The man told her she was right, he was going to the woods every evening to see another woman. After that, his wife left him and went to live with the family of one of her brothers. The man was happy because finally he was alone in the house. Now he could bring the knife home. It would no longer have to live in the hollow tree in the woods. He tore out a piece of the lining in his jacket and used it to make a fine bed for the knife next to his own on the earthen floor. Then he went to the woods to get it. When he neared the hiding place, he caught sight of the back of a man disappearing among the trees."

Lance thought about what he'd seen at the creek a few hours earlier. As if somebody had quickly retreated so he wouldn't be seen.

Willy breathed hard as he straightened up in his chair and slowly reached for the glass of water on the table. Once again Lance saw how the old man's hand shook as he raised the glass to his lips. Some of the water spilled over the side, running down his wrist and under his shirtsleeve, but Willy didn't seem to notice. When he finally managed to get the glass into position, he tilted his head back and emptied it in three big gulps. Then the glass had to travel in the opposite direction, back to its place on the table. Lance realized that all his muscles had tensed up while the whole drinking ritual was under way. Willy straightened up and pressed one hand to his stomach. Then he proceeded to belch for several seconds. Lance could smell it from the other side of the table. Finally the old Indian exhaled audibly and sank back against his chair.

"That's better," he said. "Now where were we?"

"The man was approaching the hollow tree where he'd hidden the knife," said Lance. "But someone was there."

"Yes, he saw the back of a man disappearing among the trees. He got worried, but when he looked inside the hiding place, the knife was still there. That night he was finally able to keep the knife at his side, and the next day he attached it to his belt and began using it, which was what he'd always wanted to do. Even though the knife was magic, it was still a knife. And it was a good one. He used it every single day. He cut off slices of moose meat, gutted fish, and whittled splinters of wood that he could use to light a fire in the hearth. But at night he would place the knife on the soft bed he had made for it. And there they would lie, stretched out next to each other like any other married couple.

"One day when he went down to his canoe at the lake, he again saw a man disappearing among the trees. And even though he saw him only from the back, he felt sure it was the same man he'd seen near the hollow tree. He followed him into the woods for a short way, but the man was gone. He wasn't happy about this, because he thought it had something to do with the knife. He wondered if the man might be a spirit who was looking for it. For a moment he even considered throwing the knife into the lake, but when he held it in his hand, he felt as if he were about to kill a friend, and he couldn't do it. He continued to carry it with him in the daytime, and placed it beside him when he slept at night.

"Until one day when he went over to Hat Point again to set out his nets. That was when he noticed a canoe drifting nearby. He had no idea where it had come from, because he hadn't seen or heard anyone. When the two canoes were only a stone's throw from each other, he realized the man in the other canoe was Swamper Caribou. He knew the medicine man had disappeared several months earlier. Everyone knew about it. He'd also heard that Swamper had been killed and eaten by an ice giant, a so-called *windigo*. Now he understood that it was Swamper he'd seen earlier, and it made sense that the knife belonged to the spirit world. Swamper Caribou's spirit had come to take it back.

"The man paddled for shore as fast as he could go, but the whole time he could hear the oar strokes of the other canoeist coming closer. When his canoe scraped bottom, only a few yards from shore, he jumped out and began wading toward land. But he was worn out after paddling so hard, and he slipped and fell. As he lay on his back in the shallow water, hardly able to move, he was certain the end had come. With the last of his strength he propped himself up enough on his elbows so he could look behind him. But no one was there. Nor did he see any canoe other than his own, which was several yards away.

"After that the man stopped going outside. He would lie on his bed all day long, staring at the knife that lay next to him on its own little bed made from the scrap of cloth from his jacket lining. He couldn't stop looking at it. If he tried to do something else, his mind would remain focused on the knife, and he was no longer capable of accomplishing anything. He felt himself more strongly connected to the knife than to any human being, even his own mother. He didn't understand it, nor did he have any wish to understand it. He just wanted to *feel* it. That was his only wish.

"But one day something occurred that he had long expected would happen. He was lying there looking at the knife when the door opened and Swamper Caribou stood in the doorway. The man was as frightened as anyone would be when confronted by a spirit. He lay there next to the knife, staring at the figure in the doorway. Swamper Caribou came over to the man, who could feel the blazing eyes of the medicine man on him. He knew that now he was going to lose the knife, the only true friend he had. The medicine man squatted down, picked up the knife, and studied it closely. He looked pleased and nodded to himself. Then he said, 'You have taken something that does not belong to you.' The man was so terrified to hear the spirit speak that he couldn't muster a single word in reply. 'This knife belongs to someone else. He needs it where he is now,' said the spirit. Then the medicine man stood up and calmly left the house.

"The man had survived an encounter with the spirit world, but he was completely changed. Friends and neighbors hardly recognized him. He never smiled anymore, and they soon forgot that they'd ever heard him laugh. He grew thin and his hair turned gray. Over the course of only a few weeks he had become an old man. One day in the fall he was standing on the wharf here in Grand Portage, waiting for the steamboat from Duluth. A big crowd always gathered for the arrival of the boat. Some came to meet family members or acquaintances who had gone to town; others were waiting for supplies. But most people just came to see the boat and the crowd. The man was standing there with his uncle. Neither of them had any special reason for being there. They were just watching the boat pull into the dock. That was when he caught sight of Swamper Caribou's spirit up on the deck, together with a group of passengers about to come ashore in Grand Portage. His uncle could tell something was wrong because the man kept pointing as he gawked and tried to say something, but not a word came out of his mouth. When his uncle asked him what was the matter, the man finally managed to whisper in his ear that he could see a spirit standing on the deck of the steamboat. And it wasn't just any old spirit, either. It was the spirit of Swamper Caribou. It stood alone, just to the left of the group of passengers, and it was smoking a pipe.

"But his uncle laughed loudly. 'That's Swamper Caribou's *brother* you're looking at, you miserable fool,' he said. 'Do you really think spirits travel by steamboat?' It was the brother that he'd seen all along. He was the one who had crept around in the woods, and he was the one who had come to get the knife so that the other medicine men could once again send it out onto the lake. Even though the whole mystery was finally solved, the man never returned to his former self. And he didn't get his wife back, either."

A few seconds passed before Lance realized that this was the end of the story. He had a feeling Willy was trying to tell him something about Mary, about their marriage. Maybe even something about what he'd done wrong. But what had happened had simply happened, and he was not solely to blame. That was just how things had turned out. And in the end Mary no longer wanted to live with him. She probably realized she'd chosen the wrong man. Suddenly Lance felt terribly tired. He'd been out hunting all day and had to get up early in the morning too. He glanced at his watch and saw that it was five to eleven.

"What exactly does this story have to do with your dream?" he asked.

"I forget now," replied Willy.

"You *forget?*"

Willy threw out his hands in apology. "I'm an old man," he said. "My memory isn't what it used to be."

"But why was it so important to tell me all this?"

Willy looked as if he didn't quite understand the question. "Well, you were so preoccupied with Swamper Caribou the last time you were here," he said.

"Sure, I guess so . . . ," said Lance.

"You asked me whether I knew any old stories about him. You even showed me a photograph. Or did I dream that too?"

"No, no. Of course not."

"A picture of his brother," Willy went on.

"Yeah. That's right."

"Didn't you say that one of your ancestors killed Swamper?"

"I did say that."

"Why?"

"Er, because . . . because of the coincidence of time and place. Swamper Caribou disappeared in March 1892, around the time of the full moon, which was on the sixteenth of the month."

"How do you know that?"

"It's mentioned in an issue of the *Grand Marais Pioneer* from that year. I have the Historical Society archives at home, you know. Joe Caribou, Swamper's brother, had gone to see the editor to report his brother missing. And that's where it said the full moon was on March 16."

"And what about this ancestor of yours?"

"Thormod Olson, a relative on my mother's side of the family. He arrived alone, at the age of fifteen, in March 1892. He walked across the ice at night, in the moonlight, the whole way from Duluth to where Tofte is today. In my family the story goes that he fell through the ice and then survived a long cold night in the woods."

"But you don't believe that?"

"No."

"Why not?"

Lance hesitated a few seconds before replying.

"In the historical archives there's an old diary that was written by one of my great-grandmothers. My mother's paternal grandmother. Thormod Olson finally made it to their cabin, and they nursed him back to health. But in the diary she writes that he had two deep wounds in his right arm. To me it sounds as if he had tried to defend himself from being stabbed, or something like that."

"Stabbed by Swamper Caribou?"

"Maybe."

Lance didn't mention what else he'd discovered in the diary—the fact that his great-grandmother Nanette, whom everyone had always described as French Canadian, was actually Ojibwe. Not necessarily full-blooded, but still. Andy and Lance Hansen both had Ojibwe blood in their veins. This was something that Lance hadn't told anyone.

"Then maybe it's not really so strange that I thought you should hear this story, is it?" said Willy.

"No. You did the right thing to call me."

"Besides, it's Sunday tomorrow, so you can sleep in."

"No, I can't. I'm going hunting."

"Oh, right. Because you didn't shoot anything today?"

"I *chose* not to shoot."

Lance looked down and noticed that the legs of his pants were spattered with tiny drops of blood.

"I ran over a cat. Had to kill it."

"You should wash up before you leave. You've got some blood on your face too."

"And you didn't say anything until now?"

"It doesn't bother me. But in case you stop at a gas station or something... You look like you murdered somebody."

Lance went to the bathroom and looked at himself in the mirror. Blood was sprinkled on his forehead, his nose, and his right cheek. It looked like he had freckles. How long had he pounded on that poor animal? It was as if the blows had been inside him, just waiting to get out, and he hadn't even stopped when the cat lay still. He turned on the faucet, and as he was about to put his hands under the stream of water, he saw that they, too, were spattered with blood. Fortunately nobody had seen him like this. Only Willy. He was sure about that. But then he remembered the other car, which had stopped right next to him. He had kept on bashing the cat, and after a few moments the car had driven off. Was it possible someone had recognized him? So what? He'd run over a cat and had been forced to put it out of its misery. Any responsible person would have done the same.

In the hall he put on his boots and jacket. Then he opened the door to the living room and stuck his head inside. Willy was still sitting in the same easy chair, with his hands clasped on his stomach.

"I'll be off now," he said.

"No, sit down," said Willy.

"But . . ."

"Just for a moment. You come here so seldom."

Lance went into the room and sat down again, this time wearing his jacket and boots.

"When you and Mary got divorced . . ." Willy began, but then stopped himself. After a pause he continued. "I've always considered you to be a good man, Lance. But don't you think you tend to get a bit . . . obsessed? Get totally lost in . . . well, one thing or another?"

Lance realized that he had no desire to continue this conversation.

"Isn't that true?"

"*Obsessed?* The fact that Mary and I got divorced was . . . But things are fine for everybody now, right?"

"You think so?"

"Yes, I do. Isn't everything fine? With Jimmy and Mary? They're okay, aren't they?"

"Sure, but I don't think anybody believes *you're* okay anymore."

Instead of making a joke or brushing the remark aside, Lance simply sat there, looking around the room as if searching for a peg to hang it on.

"I was wondering whether you might have become . . . obsessed with something again."

"I'm perfectly fine," said Lance.

The old man reacted with an almost imperceptible shake of his head.

Lance stood up.

"Don't go," said Willy.

"I don't have time for this," said Lance, and he left.

3

ONLY THE ROWANBERRIES, hanging in big clusters, shimmered in the gray light. Lance sat in his car, waiting for his brother. Taped to the middle of the steering wheel was a photograph of his seven-year-old son. The radio was on, but turned down too low for him to hear what was being said. A flock of waxwings was eating berries from the rowan trees that stood between the parking lot and the river. It was an annual sight in November.

He took a heart-shaped Dove chocolate out of his jacket pocket, removed the thin foil wrapper, and placed the candy on his tongue. His mouth quickly filled with the sweet taste. As always, he smoothed out the wrapper to read what it said inside.

"Your secret admirer will soon appear."

A second later Andy pulled into the parking lot. Lance got out. The air felt damp, but it wasn't raining. He opened the back of the Jeep. There lay the wrench, with a big white tuft of fur stuck to the dried blood. His rifle, a .243-caliber Savage with fiber-glass stock, was wrapped up in a brown blanket. After casting a quick glance at his brother, who was still sitting in his Chevy Blazer, Lance unwrapped his gun. Then he hid the wrench under the blanket.

Only when he heard Andy close his car door did he turn around.

"Early, aren't you?" said his brother. He had on dark green rain gear, just like Lance. And he was wearing a Minnesota Twins cap.

"Not really," replied Lance, slamming the magazine into place. Beyond the trees, where the waxwings were still stuffing themselves with rowanberries, he could see the froth on the river as it rushed past the steep slopes of the rocky section, just before the bridge. It looked like something between a waterfall and rapids. He could clearly hear the roar of the water. Below the bridge the river slowed and calmly traversed the last few hundred yards until it reached the lake down near Baraga's Cross.

"So where did you say you saw that buck in the summer?"

"Right up here." Andy opened the back of his vehicle. He took out his rifle and slung it over his shoulder. "But whether it's still around . . ."

"Is your cell phone fully charged today?"

"It's working fine."

"I sure hope so, since I can't find the walkie-talkies."

Andy looked at his brother for a moment without commenting.

"Your turn to drive?" he finally asked.

Lance nodded.

"I suppose it's natural to divide it up into shorter drives, right?" Andy went on. "Because of the power line."

"Yeah."

"And if nothing happens by the time you get there, we'll make another attempt."

"Farther up, near the big bend in the river," said Lance. "There should be some great posts in the hills over there."

He looked at his watch. "How much time do you need to get up to the power line?"

"Shall we say half an hour?" replied Andy.

LANCE MUST HAVE BEEN about ten at the time. Their father had taken the two boys along on a fishing trip, and they had borrowed a cabin. All these years later, Lance couldn't recall where it was located, but he did remember that they'd caught some fish. He had a clear memory of frying and eating the fish in the cabin at night. But that wasn't what he was thinking about as he sat in the car with his rifle beside him, waiting in the parking lot near the Cross River.

It must have been after they were done fishing. The cabin had to have been some distance away from where they'd been fishing because they'd arrived by car. It was late in the evening, but the moon shone brightly over the woods. They were planning to stop somewhere to look at the moon. But first their father had turned onto a narrow side road that was almost completely overgrown, with a ridge of tall grass between the tire ruts. Tree branches scraped over the roof of the car.

They'd walked a short way along a path, and then he saw it very clearly up ahead. The moon high above the treetops. It must have been a full moon, he thought. Or at least almost full. Yet it was so dark on the path that he had trouble making his way forward. Two dark figures were in front of him, one short and one tall, his little brother holding his dad's hand. Finally they emerged onto what looked like a viewpoint. Could it have been Carlton Peak? he wondered. But no, it must have been much farther away from Lake Superior. It was the sight of the lake that he happened to think about now. They stood there together, the father and his two sons, somewhere in the woods, at an elevated spot with a view. Their father must have taken them there to show them exactly what Lance was now thinking about. The dark forest world all around them, spreading out in every direction. Not a single electric light, only the darkness of night and the metallic gleam of the huge body of water beneath the moonlight. Surrounded by darkness, it looked like it was floating in space. How could he have forgotten *that?*

And now here he sat, half a lifetime later, out hunting with Andy. He ought to be feeling good. I like hunting, he thought, always have. But here he sat, as if in a tunnel, with the rest of the world blocked from view. A tunnel that led only one way and shut out everything else. Andy was somewhere up ahead in the tunnel. Lance wasn't sure what all these thoughts meant, but the tunnel image best described what his life was like now.

It's not much of a life, he thought. Andy was a murderer, and he himself wasn't really any better. When he lay in bed at night, unable to sleep, it was usually because he was thinking about Lenny Diver, the twenty-five-year-old Ojibwe man from Grand Portage who was in jail in Minneapolis. He'd been charged with the murder of the Norwegian canoeist Georg Lofthus. Lance knew Diver was as good as convicted even before the trial began. The murder weapon, a baseball bat with the victim's blood on it, had been found in his car. And he'd also given a phony alibi. In other words, he might as well have confessed to the whole thing. But he hadn't. On the contrary, Diver stubbornly denied being anywhere near Baraga's Cross on the night in question. And Lance believed him. He knew the baseball bat that had been found in Diver's car had the initials "AH" carved into the wood, just like on Andy's bat. And with his own eyes he'd seen his brother drive down the road to Baraga's Cross just hours before the murder occurred. The next day Andy had shown up at the ranger station and told Lance and everyone else who was there that he'd been out at his cabin on Lost Lake the previous night. He claimed to have gone out in his boat to fish and had stayed out there until midnight. But Lance knew he was lying. So he was enormously relieved when he heard that they'd arrested an Ojibwe and that the blood found at the crime scene proved the killer had to be a man with Indian blood. It had to do with a gene mutation that was found almost exclusively in American Indians.

But his relief abruptly vanished when he discovered that his great-grandmother Nanette had been Ojibwe. Which meant that the evidence from the crime scene was not conclusive when it came to determining whether Lenny Diver or Andy Hansen had committed the murder. And with that, Lance was right back where he'd started, harboring a strong suspicion that his brother was the guilty party. This knowledge had transformed Lance into a corrupt police officer who was protecting a family member from the law.

Yet even worse was the thought of Lenny Diver sitting in a cell in Minneapolis, awaiting the court trial in which he would undoubtedly be given a life sentence. He was there because Lance had not come forward with the truth. Isn't that the same thing as taking a life? he thought. A form of murder, just slower. In spite of everything, Georg Lofthus must have died quickly. For Lenny Diver, it would take the same length of time for him to lose his life inside the prison walls as it would have taken him to spend his life outside.

A half hour must have passed by now. Lance turned up the volume on the radio, which had been on the whole time but turned down so low that it was nearly inaudible. He caught the tail end of the news broadcast. A helicopter had been shot down, several soldiers had perished, but he didn't hear where this had happened.

It was eight thirty. Time to head out. He decided to do

his best to ensure that this hunting expedition was as brief as possible. Today he was going to shoot the first deer that came within range, regardless of its size or sex.

He went to the back of the Jeep to get out the small backpack that held a thermos of coffee, a bottle of water, and two chicken salad sandwiches. He slipped his arms through the straps of the backpack, then slung his rifle over his right shoulder and began walking across the parking lot toward the woods.

As soon as he got in among the low birch trees that grew at the end of the parking lot, he became covered with a thin layer of moisture, from his hair all the way down to his boots. It wasn't raining, but all the branches were laden with shiny drops. The air felt damp, like a thick mist, as he breathed it into his lungs, but there was no rain or fog. It was just an overcast November day, the kind that never gets fully light. Lance was moving slowly. Cautiously he pushed aside the branches as he tried to make his way through the trees. He wasn't especially good at this. Andy was the expert at stalking prey. But it didn't really matter, because in this dense birch forest he wouldn't be able to shoot at anything. So he kept his rifle slung over his shoulder, but he still tried to move as quietly as possible. They didn't want some deer to race past Andy's post at too high a speed. Then it would be difficult to hit. The ideal scenario was for the deer to approach at a slow pace, nervous and on guard, of course, but not panic-stricken. Like when the deer had appeared at Copper Pond yesterday. It wasn't frightened; it had simply stood there, checking the scents and the terrain. If Andy had come tramping through the woods, shouting loudly, that same deer would have been nothing but a brown streak racing across the marsh. Then Lance remembered how his brother had knocked on the window on the wrong side of the Jeep. Had he even been anywhere near Copper Pond?

He veered to the right, heading closer to the sound of the river. The source of Cross River was in the huge complex of marshes deep within the Superior National Forest. It started out as a slow-moving and meandering current, more like a wide, quiet creek. Gradually it increased in size by absorbing water from the countless other small creeks, but it continued to flow gently through the extensive, almost-level conifer forests. When only a couple of miles remained, the river took on a more impressive form. The flat, at times slightly undulating, forest landscape abruptly changed to a hilly terrain that ended down by the narrow shoreline and Highway 61. These hills finally allowed the river water to become a foaming, rushing torrent. Then, after this short but dramatic phase, the Cross River calmly flowed on for roughly two hundred yards before emptying into Lake Superior at Baraga's Cross.

Lance was still near the lower, steep part of the river. A bit higher up the water passed through several clefts, but the Cross River would never be as spectacular as, for instance, the Cascade River or the Manitou.

At one spot he found fresh deer scat. After that he was even more cautious, carrying his rifle in his hands, ready to shoot at a moment's notice. He would have preferred to happen upon a deer and get this hunt over with as quickly as possible, but from experience he knew that would be difficult. He'd never shot a deer that way, when taking the role of driver. Andy, on the other hand, had done it several times. He had no idea how his brother was able to sneak up on deer, which were such wary animals.

Where in this area would he be most likely to find a deer at this precise moment? The answer was "on the slopes along the river." He didn't ask himself why, just blindly trusted his experience, which was not simply the result of a quarter century of deer hunting but was based equally, or maybe even more, on the fact that these woods were his workplace all year round.

The river was his most important partner. Because of the high water level, he figured it was improbable that any deer would try to cross the river, which meant that the current would serve as a reliable right flank for him. He was the left flank. If he was careful to maintain a certain distance from the river, the deer would probably continue straight ahead. Ideally this would lead the animal to a lethal encounter with Andy's Winchester up near the power line. From that position he would have an unobstructed line of fire. But if Lance got too close to the river, he would remove his own left flank, and the deer might flee in that direction. So he made a point of keeping the desired distance from the river.

He suddenly became aware of a sound and then realized that it had actually been present for a while. It was the sound of rain striking his Gore-Tex clothing. At the moment it was no more than a drizzle. He pulled up his hood. This was good hunting weather. A fall day with sunshine and a cloudless sky might be beautiful, but sounds carried much farther through crisp, clear air. Smells did too. No, gray days that hovered like wet woolen blankets over the forest—those were the best. Then the chances were greater for getting close to a deer.

Lance stopped at the top of a small rise with a view of the river. He was breathing hard. He wiped the mixture of rain and sweat from his brow and proceeded to examine the terrain, in particular several clearings along the river. But he didn't see anything of interest. The only thing moving was a small flock of songbirds, apparently searching for food in the birch trees. Then the birds moved to a fir tree only a few yards away. One of them crept headfirst down along the slippery trunk. Lance knew that only a nuthatch could do that. The flock looked to be a mixture of nuthatches and black-capped chickadees, with maybe a few boreal chickadees or brown creepers.

He thought of his mother holding up the palms of her hands, the way someone does to catch the first drops of rain. They had been standing outside a small house on a secluded street in Two Harbors, where she and Lance's father had lived during the first year of their marriage. One morning she had gone to the kitchen window to look outside. It was snowing, and snow had already covered the trees and the fence. Oscar was out there feeding the birds, as he did every morning. But Inga said this time a little bird had landed on his hand. And soon more did the same. They were swarming around her husband as he stood there in the yard with the snow falling all around. When she saw how surprised Lance was to hear about this incident, Inga asked him whether he'd ever seen his father feeding birds from his hand. No, Lance had told her. His mother thought this was strange, because she said Oscar used to feed the birds in their yard in Duluth when Lance was growing up. But he couldn't recall seeing anything like that, and it had bothered him ever since. If he'd really seen his father do something as special as that, why didn't he have even the slightest memory of it? And if he'd forgotten about his father's ability to attract the birds, what else might he have forgotten?

The flock of birds now flew over to a tree farther away. How long had he been standing here, thinking about his parents? Maybe a couple of minutes. But that wasn't good. It had broken his concentration. He started walking again, but the thought of his father and the songbirds soon returned, along with the memory of the day when his mother told him the story. Afterward they had stopped at a rest area because her knees were starting to ache. And there . . . down by the lake . . . Lance had seen the back of a man sitting near the water. Apparently his mother hadn't noticed him, even though she was standing right next to Lance. An Ojibwe Indian. He didn't belong in the same world as Lance and his mother. And yet Lance had seen him. He looked as if he'd wandered out of a black-and-white photograph from sometime around 1900. And Lance knew who he was. It was Swamper Caribou.

A shot rang out in the woods. It came from the correct direction. Andy had fired a shot. Lance raised his rifle to chest level and stared at the clearings down by the river. If his brother had missed, it was conceivable that the deer might turn around and run back, away from the gunfire. In that case, it would pass very close to where Lance was standing. But if his brother had brought the deer down, he would soon call on his cell to say so.

But nothing else happened. No deer came bounding past, no more shots were fired, his cell phone didn't start vibrating. Andy must have missed, and then the deer took off in another direction.

Lance lowered his rifle and began walking again, on the alert the whole time. Maybe Andy had hit the deer but didn't kill it. Sometimes merely wounding an animal couldn't be helped. Soon he'd reach the power line. Before he got there, he had to call Andy to warn him, but for the next few minutes he could still focus all his attention on the hunt.

He enjoyed the supremely goal-oriented nature of hunting. The fact that everything he heard and saw was important. That each step he took, and the way he moved, counted. That everything had significance. And yet almost nothing happened. Maybe he saw a flock of nuthatches. Maybe he heard a pinecone fall. An entire day could pass in that fashion. It was almost like experiencing a great, liberating nothingness. But then all of a sudden, in the midst of that nothingness, a deer might be standing there, on alert, its long ears moving like remote-controlled antennas. Then it all came down to a few seconds of deliberate action. As if all of existence had been kneaded into a compact little ball. And when he fired, he also shot a hole in that ball, and then everything once again resumed its usual dimensions. Although not quickly. It was true that it took time. But slowly the day would return to normal. Gradually his hands would stop shaking from adrenaline. The deer would lie there, steaming on the ground.

He got out his cell and phoned his brother.

"Yep," said Andy.

"Was that you shooting?"

"Yeah, but it was moving at a helluva speed. I missed. Was it you that flushed it out?"

"I don't think so. I was driving really cautiously, so . . ."

"Have you noticed anyone else in the area?"

"No."

"Me neither."

"Well . . . regardless . . . I'll be there soon."

"Okay," said Andy and ended the call.

Lance picked up his pace, no longer trying to move quietly. Soon he reached the clear-cut for the transmission line, which was mostly low shrubs and heath-covered ground. He walked forward and then stopped in the middle of the open landscape as he looked for Andy, but he didn't see him. The high-voltage lines hummed overhead. For a moment he wondered where the power line came from. He realized he'd never asked himself that question before, no matter how many times he'd looked at it. It was just a power line, buzzing with energy. He had no idea where it came from or where it ended.

"Hello?" he shouted, raising one arm in the air.

His brother had to be able to see him, standing out here in the open. The transmission line clear-cut was well over a hundred feet wide, stretching as far he could see in both directions. There wasn't even a bush that reached much higher than his knees. He must stick up like a lighthouse.

"Hello?" he shouted again. Still nothing but silence all around him.

Vapor issued from his mouth in a thick cloud each time he exhaled. He noticed that it was also rising from the neck of his jacket, from his warm body under the Gore-Tex. He thought about the buck that he'd aimed at yesterday, how the steam had risen from its body as it stood there in the rain on the other side of Copper Pond. He should have shot it; then he wouldn't have needed to come out here to the woods with Andy today. But it was too late now.

Again he looked all around, letting his gaze survey a small section at a time, just as he usually did when searching for a deer. That was when he caught sight of his brother on the other side of the clear-cut strip. Partially hidden behind a fir tree, Andy was standing there, watching him.

It's impossible to cross the creek. I'll just have to follow it through the woods to see if it gets any narrower. I don't like this dark forest. I just don't. Back home we had hardly any forests. The trees that we did have stood far apart. Here it's nothing but miserable darkness. I start walking along the creek and reach the first of the fir trees. I didn't know there were trees this big anywhere. If I try to see the tops of them, it's like the whole vault of the sky comes plunging down on my head. They're trees and yet they're something else too. They're too big to be just trees. I walk in between them. The trunks are so thick it would take at least three men to link hands around them. I hear water running in the dark. That cursed creek! I say. But my words fall straight down to the hard-packed snow. The sounds don't travel even a few feet

*in this forest. But I still carry them inside me. There I can
think about the old words from back home.*

*I hear the water but I can't see it. I have to be careful about
setting down one foot in front of the other. Then I fall. I
land hard on my side and lie still. I lie there looking up
through the tall fir trees. It hurts bad. Way overhead I catch
a glimpse of a star. Did I break something? I mustn't injure
myself now. There can't be more than a few hours left. From
the boat shed it's supposed to be a straight path up to the
log cabin where my uncle and Nanette live. But here I lie,
with my ribs hurting. The trees don't look like trees. They
disappear up there among the stars. And on the other side
of the stars they keep growing to form another forest. There
the sky is blue and sunlight glitters on the lake. Tiny glints of
sun flash across the surface of the water, almost like sparks
from a fire. A fire in the middle of the night. I hear a snap
every time a spark flies out into the darkness. Those dry,
sharp snaps echo inside my skull. It's more beautiful than
anything I've ever seen before. It's red and green and white
and yellow. And it crackles as if somebody had tossed tiny
pebbles into my mouth.*

*I try spitting. My mouth is full of those pebbles. It's almost
impossible to spit them out. But then I realize that they're
not really stones. I open my eyes and see that I've fallen
asleep with my mouth pressed against the crusted snow. As
I prop myself up, I tear the skin right off my lips. I scream
loudly and put my hand over my mouth. Blood warms my
hand. I scream again because it hurts so bad. My lips are
still lying on the snow, frozen to the ice. I can't see them,
but I know they're lying there somewhere. I get to my feet,*

hunching forward to cradle the part that hurts. I feel warm blood running down my chin and neck. My lips are gone. They're lying in the snow among the fir trees. My whole face is stinging with frost. I went into the woods in order to cross the creek, and then I fell. That's what happened. And I fell asleep. Dreamed about another forest, up in the sky. Good Lord, I don't want to die! Not now. Only a few more hours and then it will be over. Then I will have arrived in America at last. I try to shout the word "America!" But with my bleeding mouth it comes out like the lowing of a cow.

I hear the creek again. The sound is more muted. Could it be that the water is running underneath the ice? It's only a few yards away, but it's so dark here. I set one foot in front of the other, moving slowly, one step at a time. The ground is uneven, and it hurts to walk. But then I see the creek! The moonlight reaches all the way down through the trees at this spot. A big patch of light. The snow sinks down into the creek bed and then rises up again on the other side. I can't see any open water at all. But I know that I don't dare trudge down into it. If I fall through the snow and into the water, I'm done for. But in the middle I see what looks like a skull sticking up. It must be a rock in the middle of the creek. It would be easy enough to jump across here in the daylight. I'd just need to land on the rock with my right foot, and then I could leap across to the other side.

It's worse in the moonlight. Then you can't really see how high or low anything is. But there's no way to go around. I'll have to gamble everything on landing on that rock with my right foot. First I have to make sure my knapsack is strapped properly on my back. I try to forget about what's hurting me. Because it really does hurt. Both my face and my side. But I need to forget about that. Right now all that matters is the creek. Me and the creek. I walk all the way over to the edge, or what I think is the edge, and try to judge the distance, but that's hard to do in the moonlight. Then I take off from my left foot, launching myself forward with my right leg out. I touch down on the round shape sticking up in the middle of the creek, and instinctively throw my left leg out, not thinking about whether I can do it or not. I just do it, and then I'm lying on the other side, digging my fingers into the hard-packed snow. My knapsack and snowshoes have slid forward and are lying on top of my head. Cautiously I turn onto my side and see that I've made it across.

Now it's just a matter of following the creek down to the lake, and then I can keep going like before. But I won't be able to handle many more creeks. Not with this sharp pain in my side. It hurts terribly now, after jumping like that. I really must have cracked something. Maybe a rib. But that's not so dangerous, is it? A person can't die from a broken rib. I get up on my knees. Something scrapes and stabs inside me. But I have to get up. All the way up. I scream, it hurts so bad. I try to scream "America!" but it just comes out the same way, a crazy lowing sound, because my lips are still lying on the other side of the creek.

I start walking toward the lake, going much slower now. Every time I lift my left foot, something scrapes inside me. A broken rib. But I can't let something stupid like that stop me. Soon I'll arrive where my uncle and Nanette are living. I pause. Tip my head back and look up. I see a star. The trees are too big to be just trees. I'm being sucked up between them. High above the treetops I don't feel how much it hurts. My old life is on the other side of the ocean, just like my lips are on the other side of the creek. One day I happened to read a letter from my uncle, about the big lake and all the money that could be made. After that I couldn't think of anything but America. But I'm not quite there yet. First I need to smell the food cooking and the heat coming from the cabin where Knut lives. Right now I'm sitting on the ground again. I must have fallen. I need to get up and head down to the lake. I'm not going to get any porridge or coffee this way. But I have a terrible pain inside me. I stand up and start walking, groaning out loud with each step I take. Up ahead I can see the lake between the tree trunks. The black water. The moonlight.

IT HAD STOPPED RAINING. Lance could hear the sound of rushing water being squeezed between the cliff walls in the narrow gap a short distance away, off to the right. The river was still at his right flank, but this was a longer drive than the first, so the chances were greater that a deer might break out of this one. He had no idea where the deer had come from on the first drive. But he had definitely not flushed it out. Regardless, his brother had missed. And from what Andy had said, he hadn't wounded the deer. They hadn't found any traces of blood either.

Although it might seem like he was the only living thing here, Lance knew there was plenty of life all around him. Nuthatches, woodpeckers, hazel grouse, hares, and squirrels. There might also be mink and otters along the river. And deer, of course. Yet the landscape appeared utterly dead. Even the birches looked dead as they stood there, leafless and covered with shiny droplets. He didn't hear a single sound that might be ascribed to a human being or to a man-made object. As soon as he got a short distance away from any houses and roads, the only sounds were the ones that had always been present. Gusts of wind, river water, rain, maybe the snapping of a twig. If he closed his eyes and listened, he could have been the first Frenchman who'd ever set foot in the woods surrounding Lake Superior. He stopped and closed his eyes, shutting out all sight of himself, the modern sports clothing, the rifle with the fiberglass stock. He heard only the roar of the river and the sound of his own breathing. Felt the cold, damp air on his hands and face, noticed the smell of rotting vegetation and wet earth.

He opened his eyes and checked to make sure his cell phone was pressed against his thigh so that he'd notice if it started to vibrate. Then he slowly began walking again. The same wet woods. The same rotting leaves on the ground. The same low-hanging, leaden sky cover.

Why hadn't Andy answered when he was standing out there shouting in the transmission line clear-cut? Instead he'd stood half-hidden among some fir trees, watching him. It reminded Lance of yesterday, when Andy hadn't picked up any of his calls.

A blue jay flew out from a spruce tree. A swift glimpse of its iridescent blue feathers and then it was gone, as if it had never been there.

Lance still had a long way to go to reach the big bend in the river where Andy was on post. A long, steep climb. This was a hard drive. Once again Lance felt annoyed with himself because he hadn't shot that buck yesterday. If he had, he could be sitting at home right now. Not that he knew what he'd be doing if he were, but at least he could have avoided spending the day out here in the woods with Andy.

Had he gone too far from the river? Lance stopped to listen. The roar of the water was fainter. But that could also be the fault of some big evergreens, or a small rise in the terrain might be blocking the sound. He veered to the right, heading for the river. Soon he could see it. And at that spot the river curved.

A bald eagle was perched in a fir tree on the other side. Lance raised his rifle to look at it through the scope. There was always something solemn about eagles, he thought, no matter how often he saw them. Only in the very depths of winter, from Christmastime until mid-February, was the North Shore more or less bereft of eagles. But it hadn't always been like that.

Lance had a vivid memory of the first time he ever saw a bald eagle. He was with his family on a driving vacation in Manitoba, Canada. When they parked at a rest area near a big river, they'd caught sight of an eagle sitting on a rock in the water. What a commotion that caused! He and Andy had almost come to blows, competing for their dad's binoculars. And when the bird finally took off, flying low over the river with almost unreal flaps of his big, heavy wings, all four of them had cheered and clapped. That was how rare the sight of a bald eagle had been in the early 1970s.

Lance lowered his rifle. With the naked eye he could still see the bird clearly. Its neck and head gleamed snow white in the gray November light. He hadn't been too far from the river after all. It was this curve in the riverbed that had altered the sound of the current slightly. Now he moved off to the west at a diagonal, away from Cross River again.

Seeing the eagle in his rifle scope made him think of other driving vacations. The family's old Dodge Dart, which was always filled with smoke from his father's cigarettes. His mother desperately trying to smooth out the map, and his father shoving it aside with annoyance as he tried to see where he was driving. The two brothers in the backseat passed the time reading comic books and thinking up competitive games. For example, who could come up with the most baseball players whose names started with the letter *A*. Then *B*. Then *C*. And on through the whole damn alphabet. Or who could count the most cows on "his" side of the road all the way through Wisconsin. Or how long would it take before Dad lit up another cigarette? Things like that. Once in a while they'd start hitting each other until their father told them to shut up and sit still.

What was it about Andy when he was a kid? Because there had definitely been something going on, but they never asked him. Not even why he'd beat up Clayton Miller, the boy everyone said was gay. Peaceful, shy Andy. Their parents must have been just as shocked as Lance was, yet they'd never talked about it. The incident had come right out of the blue, and no doubt it was best if it disappeared the same way. That was what all of them had thought. What they feared more than anything else was the *unpleasantness*. To avoid that, they preferred to let Andy keep his reasons to himself. What he'd done was bad enough. Talking about *why* he did it would have been unbearable. But what if it had been a different kid instead of Clayton? Would the episode have been equally unpleasant? It wasn't unusual for high school boys to fight, was it? No, but in this case it was Clayton Miller, the kid who reportedly knitted his own scarves. Who the hell knits his own scarves? thought Lance, annoyed. But there was something about Andy that was also to blame. Something they'd never talked about. Of course they wouldn't talk about it! Good Lord, they didn't even *think* about such things back then. At least Lance couldn't recall ever thinking about it before.

But now, now that it was way too late, he saw what it was: there had always been a certain *ambiguity* about his brother. As if the substance he was made of had never hardened in the mold but had remained in a liquid state. He was not like his peers. It was impossible to know what Andy liked, what he wished for, where he was headed. By now he was completely changed, but Lance had never noticed this transformation taking place. For the most part they had lost contact with each other years ago, and the deer hunting was the one thing that remained. Somewhere along the way the ambiguous and slightly odd Andy from their youth had become the man who was now on post up near the big bend in the river. Tammy's grouchy husband, and seventeen-year-old Chrissy's father.

It had started raining again. Lance pulled up the hood of his Gore-Tex jacket. The sound of the raindrops on the synthetic fabric reminded him of the nights they'd slept in a tent as kids. He and Andy would lie awake all night out in the backyard of their house in Duluth, listening to the sounds. The rain on the tent canvas. The passing cars. Voices in the dark. No, he didn't want to think about that. As soon as this hunt was over, he would never again go out in the woods with his brother. He didn't care what the rest of the family thought. After today, it was over. The last thing that had connected them was about to become history.

But there was something else that now bound them together. A bond that could never be broken. The knowledge of a murder. And the guilt. They were both guilty of robbing Lenny Diver of his life every single day. Regardless of whether Lance ever went hunting with Andy again, he and his brother were bound to each other by an unbreakable bond. And they were the only two who knew it.

Up ahead a flash of white appeared through the rain. It took only seconds before hail came pounding down, and Lance's field of vision shrank to twenty or thirty yards. Then it was like someone had turned on the faucet full blast. He could no longer see even an arm's length in front of him. He stopped, bent his head forward, and hunched his shoulders. It sounded like a landslide of gravel. The ground underfoot remained dark. The hail disappeared in the grass and heath. After a couple of minutes it once again turned to rain.

Lance continued walking. When he got to the top of a small hill, he paused to look around. He had a feeling something was going to happen very soon. With an experienced eye he surveyed the terrain. He needed to take one small area at a time—that was the secret. Not let his eyes jump around at random, because then he was certain to miss something. It was a matter of examining the landscape piece by piece, just as he was doing now.

As he shifted his gaze toward a clearing in the woods, about a hundred yards away, he saw the back and shoulders of a man disappearing between several tall spruce trees. The figure was visible for only a fraction of a second, and yet Lance had no doubt what he'd just seen. There weren't supposed to be any other hunters around here. Not this weekend. The stretch of land along the lower section of Cross River was part of the area covered by the Hansen brothers' hunting licenses. But this was a potentially dangerous situation, and he'd have to call Andy to tell him. They were going to have to stop the drive. He got out his phone and was about to tap in the number, but then he hesitated. It was still a good distance up to where Andy was waiting on post. What if he followed this man to see which direction he was headed? Andy had already fired at a buck without hitting it. There were obviously deer in the area, and Lance wanted to get this hunting expedition over with as quickly as possible. If they stopped now, he couldn't say how things would go.

He walked quickly toward the clearing where he'd seen the man, but he was as intent as always about proceeding cautiously. Still holding his rifle in his hands, ready to shoot, he walked between the conifers. The man had gone toward the river. Why was he so sure that it was a man? It had happened so fast. But what would a woman be doing out here?

Lance had also caught a glimpse of a man yesterday. Or had he? He wasn't sure what he'd actually seen near the creek coming from Copper Pond. A person who had swiftly retreated. That had been his first impression. But now? No, he was no longer sure.

The light was dim here among the huge spruce trees, as if dusk were already approaching. He stopped to listen but heard only the muted roar of the river. Thick tree trunks surrounded him on all sides. This was one of the sections of old-growth forest in this part of the Superior National Forest. To find trees of this size anywhere else, you'd have to go all the way up to the totally protected wilderness, up near the Canadian border. Lance didn't know why this pocket of timber was still here. Some of the trees had to be well over a hundred years old.

He continued on toward the river. Maybe he'd be able to catch sight of the man there. If not, he'd have to make a decision. The sound of the water increased dramatically, and soon he was standing on the edge of a deep river gully. There couldn't be more than a couple of yards between the cliff walls, and water was thundering violently through the narrow gap. His face got wet from the spray shooting up from the depths below. A little farther up he could see big rocks sticking out of the water, and it looked like it might be possible to cross the river at that point. When he went over there to get a closer look, he saw at once that it couldn't be done. So the man must still be on this side of the river. The same side where Lance and Andy were hunting.

What should he do? They had never before failed to shoot the one deer they were allowed on the second weekend in November. If that happened now, Lance wouldn't be able to refuse to go hunting the following weekend. If he did, that would make Andy even more suspicious than he already was. He clearly suspected that Lance was behind the break-in at his cabin this past summer. If Lance now refused to finish the hunt, Andy would take it as a final confirmation that his brother was keeping something from him. But did he know *what* Lance was hiding?

Does he know that I know? he thought.

The man had most likely followed the river down the slope and was now on his way toward Highway 61. It seemed highly unlikely that he would end up anywhere near where Andy was posted. Lance decided to continue on as if nothing had happened, and yet he felt slightly uneasy as he went back into the old-growth forest. Now a third person had entered the picture. A stranger. And he had no idea where the man was at this moment. If anything happened, Lance would bear the brunt of responsibility. Yet he still didn't phone Andy to tell him what he'd seen. He just wanted to get this hunt over with. Then he'd have a whole year to think up an acceptable excuse for why he didn't want to go hunting anymore. This was the last time. He didn't care what the rest of the family thought. He was going to turn his back on his brother for good. Never look at his face again.

It was as if the huge spruces belonged to another era, and in some sense they did. They had probably taken root toward the end of the nineteenth century. Slender saplings in a forest that had never been logged. And here they still stood, those same trees, only many times bigger, a measure of the years that had since passed. The fact that it was so much darker in here only reinforced the feeling of isolation.

Lance placed his hand on one of the thick, gray tree trunks. How strange that it was a living being. He never used to think like that. He was a forest cop. And yet, inside this hard, rough bark he was leaning against there was a life that had already existed for more than a hundred years. Because it is a life, he thought. Maybe not conscious, but still a life. And the same was true of all the other trees surrounding him. It was perfectly obvious and yet overwhelming. More than a hundred Minnesota winters. All that snow. The blizzards. The cold that made the wood split with a sharp crack, like the sound of a gunshot through the woods. Yet they were still standing here, and as long as no one cut them down, they would most likely continue to stand here for years to come. The trees belonged as much in this moment as they did in a winter night a hundred years ago. As if he were standing in the midst of an expansive *now* that included much more than this one gray November day.

He emerged from the old-growth forest. All around him were mostly birches and shorter spruce trees. He didn't have far to go to reach Andy. He'd find a spot with a view and try to catch sight of the man he'd just glimpsed in the woods.

A little farther along, Lance saw a big boulder that looked like it would provide a good view. He hurried up the slope. When he reached the top, he realized he would have to put down his rifle in order to climb up onto the boulder. He wasn't happy about that. To be out on a hunt without ready access to his gun was not a situation any hunter relished, but if Lance wanted to go up there, he had to leave his rifle behind. He set it down at the base of the boulder and then clambered up.

The view was even better than he'd expected. Of course a lot of the terrain was covered with stunted birch woods, but the trees had all lost their leaves, so he had a bare forest ahead of him. It should be possible to spot a person among those trees. He straightened his back and began surveying the terrain. He took his time, but he didn't see anyone. Nor did he see any deer, fortunately. It would have been annoying to have a chance to put an end to the hunt while his rifle was beyond his reach.

He was just about to climb down when he suddenly

had a feeling someone was watching him. A metallic taste rose up into his mouth. Without even thinking, he jumped down in one big leap. As he landed, one knee came up and slammed into his jaw, rattling his teeth. But he didn't care as he pressed his body as close as possible against the boulder. His heart was pounding wildly. He grabbed the rifle and placed it on his lap. It felt better to be sitting in the shelter of the huge rock, having the solid stone at his back. What exactly just happened? A sudden feeling someone was looking at him. As if an ancient instinct had been triggered. A warning from deep inside him, a place with which he seldom had any contact. But a warning about what? *Someone was aiming at me,* he thought. The idea just dropped into his mind. He'd been standing on top of the boulder, visible from a wide area, and somebody had taken aim at him.

The boulder slanted a bit forward at the spot where he was sitting, so that he had a partial roof above him, as well as the wall behind his back. At the moment he felt very protected. His dark green clothing would be barely visible against the dark rock, so no one would be able to see him here. On the other hand, his own field of vision was very restricted, and he didn't like that. It would be easy for someone to sneak up on him as he hid here next to the boulder.

"Your secret admirer will soon appear."

He got up, holding the rifle in his hands, and peered around nervously, but there was nothing out of the ordinary to see. Then he started walking again. He thought he could walk the nervousness out of his system, so he strode up the slope, but it didn't do any good. The adrenaline continued to rush through his body at an unpleasant speed. A couple of times he stopped and held his hand out in front of him. It was shaking. He told himself that he needed to focus on the hunt. If a deer appeared, he'd have only a few seconds. If his mind were elsewhere, he wouldn't have a chance. And of course nobody was aiming at him.

It couldn't be very far to the bend in the river where Andy was supposed to be waiting on post. Maybe he should take the opportunity to follow the riverbank the rest of the way, even though that wasn't what he had planned. If he happened to spook a deer near the river, there was a big risk that it would flee to the left and never make it over to where Andy was waiting. At the same time, Lance had no desire to go wandering around in search of his brother, nor did he want to call him until it was necessary. If he followed the riverbank, he'd see the bend well before he came to it.

When he again reached the river, he saw that he was closer to the bend than he'd thought. It couldn't be more than a few hundred yards away, but first he had to go up a slope and walk alongside a waterfall that rushed, foaming, down the hillside. It was hard to get any traction in the wet grass, even wearing hunting boots with nonskid soles. He ended up having to use his hands, so that he was crawling upward on all fours, almost like an animal. After conquering the slope, he stood up and looked around. Up here the river was flowing, calm and dark, in a big curve. Along the entire curve the riverbank was very steep, overgrown with grass and raspberry bushes. He let his gaze sweep over the edge of the woods, but he didn't see Andy. Finally he raised one hand in the air and shouted his name. A second later he saw his brother stand up over there.

4

LANCE SPREAD OUT the ground cloth and sat down with his back resting against the rotten tree trunk. Andy sat down next to him. Each of them took out a thermos and poured coffee into a plastic cup. The aroma of coffee slowly mixed with the smell of the damp autumn forest. Both men wrapped their fingers around the cups to warm their hands.

"Oh well . . . ," Andy said, sighing.

"Uh-huh," said Lance, his voice barely audible.

Only a few yards from their feet the Cross River ran past, on its way toward the ravines and rapids. This big bend in the river marked the end of its lengthy, calm phase. But Lance and Andy had come from the opposite direction. They had left the hillsides behind on their way up from the lake. Ahead of them loomed the enormous forests that extended far into Canada, but there was no reason for them to go there today. The deer mostly kept to the hilly areas in the south.

The two brothers sat there, leaning against the trunk of a huge tree that had apparently toppled over in a storm long ago. Three feet or so separated them. Lance could hear Andy breathing, as well as the moist sound when he occasionally inhaled especially deeply through his nose.

"So, how's this all going to end?" asked Andy.

"What do you mean?"

"This . . ." He let his gaze sweep over the area.

"Oh, we'll probably get one eventually."

"You think so?"

"We always do."

"Yeah, you're right about that," said Andy. He took a bottle of milk out of his backpack, unscrewed the cap, and poured some into his coffee. Then he put the cap back on and set the bottle on the ground. "I think I'll have something to eat."

"Me too," said Lance.

Andy pushed up the sleeve of his jacket to look at his watch. "But we'll have another snack later on, right?"

"Sure. How about when we get back to the cars?"

"It all depends," said Andy.

Lance unwrapped one of his chicken salad sandwiches and took a bite. Andy picked up the milk bottle and took a big swig before setting it down again. Then he got out a Snickers bar.

Lance looked at the milk bottle with the beautiful Indian maiden on the label. She was kneeling in front of an artificially blue lake, holding out a package of butter, as if presenting a precious gift or making an offering. When he was a kid, he'd dreamed about being able to step inside the picture on Land O'Lakes products. Step right in, as if crossing a threshold, to join the beautiful Land O'Lakes maiden holding out the package of butter. And from there he would enter the picture on the butter package, to join the same maiden who was holding out the same butter in front of the same lake, which was more beautiful than any real lake he'd ever seen. Once inside, he'd enter the next picture. And so on. Each time he would join the same Indian maiden who was kneeling and holding out the same package that had exactly the same picture on the label. As if there always existed yet another world beyond that one.

But he'd also had other dreams linked to her; he remembered that now. Romantic dreams about canoe trips and wilderness adventures. A beautiful, dark-haired girlfriend. He supposed it must have been a form of love. A child's infatuation. Countless times he'd sat at the breakfast table, thinking secret thoughts about the Land O'Lakes maiden, with Andy sitting across from him and their father seated at the head of the table, hidden behind the *Duluth News-Tribune.*

What about their mother? Lance couldn't recall ever seeing her sitting at the table and eating. She was always busy with something somewhere else in the room.

"Do you remember Dad feeding the birds?" Lance asked.

"Sure," replied Andy, without looking at him.

"But do you remember seeing the birds eat out of his hand?"

"No . . . Who told you that?"

"Mom did. She said that's what he used to . . ." He broke off a piece of his sandwich and held it out, in the palm of his hand. "Like this," he added.

Andy looked at him in disbelief. "Do you really think Dad had the patience for something like that?"

"Maybe not."

"I'll be damned if he had the patience for—"

"No," said Lance. "No, you're right. That's what I thought too."

"I can just picture it," said Andy. He held out his hand as Lance had done. *"Come on and eat, and be quick about it, you fucking ungrateful little birds!"*

In his mind Lance saw the two figures, one small and one big, holding each other's hands. The moon over the lake.

Everything around them dark. Only the immense surface of the water gleaming like metal beneath the moon, as if it were the only thing in existence.

"You should show some respect for the dead," he said.

"Isn't it more important to respect the living?"

"Andy, I'm talking about our father."

"No, you mean *your* father. I'm talking about *mine.*"

They sat in silence for a while, sitting next to each other, leaning against the toppled tree trunk. The minutes passed and neither of them said a word. The river continued to flow past them, on its way to the lake. Occasionally there was a rustling sound from their rain gear if one of them moved. A little bird flew over the river and into the woods on the other side. Lance was feeling uncomfortable. They usually never sat like this. Or rather, they did, but only when they were out hunting. Even more time might go by before either of them spoke. But there had never before been such a sense of something enormous and unpredictable between them, like now. It was almost tangible. Normally they didn't talk much when they were together simply because they had nothing to say. But now it was because neither of them dared speak. Who knew what might happen once they got into what lay between them? Who could predict where they'd end up then?

Andy must be wondering why Lance hadn't called on his cell phone before he arrived. Maybe he realized it was because his brother had come walking along the river, in clear view. But why didn't he ask? Lance again tried to picture the stranger he'd seen, but it had happened so fast, and he'd seen only the man's shoulders and back. His dark green clothing. Andy was wearing dark green rain gear. Lance was too. Probably most everybody else was, too, if they were walking around in the woods today. He thought about the story Willy Dupree had told him last night. About the man who found a knife and became so attached to it that he chased away his own wife so that he could keep the knife at his side. When he went to get it from its hiding place, he saw *the back of a man who disappeared among the trees.* But it was stupid to draw an old story into what was happening here and now. Or was it? Lance had never believed in ghosts, but during the past few months he'd had several strange experiences. As if someone were walking past on the other side of a thin curtain. And it was always the same man: Swamper Caribou. Lance didn't understand it, but he would still never believe in ghosts.

Andy was staring straight ahead, his face impassive. He seems worn out, thought Lance. Really, really worn out. Does he dream about it? he wondered. Was that why he looked so tired? Because he kept waking up from the same nightmare? How many times did he raise the baseball bat to strike a blow? What had driven him to do it? Lance himself had stood there only a few hours later, staring at the shattered head of the Norwegian canoeist Georg Lofthus. Somehow Andy had managed to get Lenny Diver's fingerprints on the bat and then he hid it in the Indian's car. Maybe he'd found Lenny in a drunken stupor. Diver claimed he'd been so drunk that he couldn't remember anything about that night except for the fact that he'd ended up in a Grand Marais motel room with a woman whom he could neither describe nor name. None of the employees at any of the motels in Grand Marais had seen Lenny Diver, but that didn't mean he hadn't been there.

"Do you still have your old baseball bat?" asked Lance.

"Yeah."

"How about a game someday?"

Andy raised his eyebrows in surprise.

"I thought it'd be fun for Jimmy. Play a little ball with his dad and Uncle Andy."

"In November?"

"It'd be good for him. The boy needs to toughen up. He's growing up with only his mother, you know."

"But don't you have your own baseball bat?"

"Can't find it," replied Lance. "But I figured you'd still have that good old bat of yours."

"Actually, I'm not exactly sure where it is," said Andy.

"Maybe you . . . *left* it somewhere?" Lance gave him a cold look.

"Oh, that's right," said Andy, as if a light had come on in his brain. "I left it at the cabin. Those kids who broke in must have taken it."

He looked pleased as he poured himself some more coffee, splashing a little milk into his cup. Lance felt as if his brother was always one step ahead of him. He always seemed to have another card up his sleeve.

"I saw Chrissy in the summer," said Lance. "In Duluth. I've got to say she's changed a lot since the last time I saw her. That black hair and . . . Well, just in general."

"It's that age," said Andy.

"I saw her in Enger Park. She was with two other girls, and they were talking to somebody who was sitting in a car."

"Oh, really?"

"Well . . . I guess she never goes out to the cabin, does she?"

"No."

Now Andy seemed to be on guard. Lance sensed that he was standing right on the brink of something. He thought about the music magazine he'd found in Andy's cabin when he broke in. He couldn't imagine anyone except Chrissy taking the magazine there. Truth be told, he thought both father and daughter had been there together on the night of the murder, when Chrissy was supposedly staying over-night with a girlfriend in Duluth.

"Hey, Lance," said Andy.

"Yeah?"

"Lay off Chrissy, okay?"

"What do you mean?"

"Just lay off."

I'm standing on the big blue surface. The moon is shining. I'm frozen in place. Around me I can hear the whole bay creaking and singing. There's no way back. No way forward either. If I move, the ice will instantly shatter. I'm sure of that. Soon the darkness will open up beneath me. I don't dare move except to turn my head a little and look across the lake. It was stupid to try walking across the bay. Straight ahead I can see black water and a band of moonlight. At the very head of the bay a river is emptying into the water. So I can't trust the ice. But I did trust it. Up until it was too late. The ice is starting to crack, I felt it give a little and heard water burbling across it someplace, but I couldn't see where.

I don't want to die here! I'm supposed to look for work in the woods. Do some logging. And make some money so that I can buy my own boat. The ax! It's in my knapsack. Can I get it out without breaking through the ice? Cautiously I wriggle out of the straps of my knapsack that still has the snowshoes hanging from it. The knapsack my father gave me before I left. The handle of the ax is sticking out of it. I untie the cords as fast as I can with my stiff, cold fingers, and grip the handle as if it were my salvation. I set down the knapsack and the snowshoes. I need to hold tight to the ax when I fall through. Maybe I can use it to get back up onto the ice. Up ahead I see a spit of land with a tree standing at the very tip. Just one. I need to look for that tree if I manage to get back up onto the ice. That's where I need to go. But I now see that it doesn't look like a tree.

It looks like a cross. Maybe a grave. As if somebody has been buried there.

Suddenly the ice sinks beneath me. I keep screaming even when it stops. I'm still standing here, but water is pouring across the ice. It rises up around my boots. It's going to happen now. I'm going to fall through. Into the deep. Into the darkness. I hold the ax tight. Oh, good Lord! Oh, Jesus! Mother! I'm falling in. I flail my arms, but the water is so heavy that it won't let me go. There's no light down here. I can't tell which way is up or down. My ears hurt. I'm kicking and thrashing. Everything inside me wants out, but there is no out. Everything is black inside. I kick hard. At least I think I'm kicking hard, but I'm not sure. I'm kicking hard in the painful darkness. The dark lets go. I slip through a crack as if I've been inside the big eye of someone who was asleep and now wakes up and opens his eyes. I slide out through a half-open eye. A bright crack. A blue light. I'm still holding the ax in my right hand. And a star is shining above the blue iceberg. Shining cold and clear. It's not so bad here. I could stay here, couldn't I? I'm rising up so nicely toward the sky above the icebergs. Rising toward the star up there. It's shining so white. That's where I'm going. But now I bang my head against the star, which shatters into a thousand pieces. They clink all around me. Water is running out of the vault of the sky. Is that the moon I see? I see a man far away. He's wearing a black hat. I see a cross. Then I fall into the depths, into the deep sky above me. I see nothing, feel only this falling sensation, and I hear a voice saying, "everything that's needed for sustenance in life, such as food, drink, clothing, shoes, shelter, home, fields, cattle, money."

I am a star in the vault of the sky. Just a tiny speck twinkling high above. I can see the whole world from here. There is nothing but dark forest and snow-white water and marsh-land. A big lake that looks like a black tablecloth in the middle of it all. There is a cross at the very tip of a head-land. A man is sticking out of a hole in the ice. Just his head and arms. In one hand he is holding an ax. The man with the black hat throws something to him. It falls onto the ice, lifeless, and stays there. The man in the hole doesn't move. He simply hangs there, with his arms on top of the ice. The other man hauls back what he had thrown. He gathers it into his hands. Then he begins making his way out across the ice, hunched over, moving sideways, like a crab. I can hear him talking, but it's impossible to understand what he's saying. Nothing but sounds. Snorting. A low-pitched calling. Now he stops, preparing to throw something again. It comes rushing through the air and lands right in front of me. But I can't move even a finger. I am just hanging here, in the middle of the vaulted sky, together with the other stars, watching what's going on down below. The crab man shouts loudly several times, but nothing happens. The man sticking out of the hole in the ice doesn't move at all. And now the shapeless four-legged creature slowly starts moving forward again. This time he doesn't stop until he reaches the man in the ice. He smells of animals and smoke from a fire.

Another star grabs me around the waist. I'm being dragged across the sky. A creaking sound all around me. I feel like I'm going to throw up but can't manage to turn my head. I can't open my hand that's holding the ax. I hear someone talking behind me. It sounds like something from a dream. But this is a dream! I'm dreaming that I'm a star being dragged across the sky by another star. But that can't be right. Because now I do throw up. Vomit and water on my cheek. Am I being dragged across the snow? Across the ice? I can see the stars and the moon high overhead. I guess I'm not a star after all. I can't breathe. I thrash from side to side and throw up.

Someone is shouting. I turn my head and see the black crab over there. He's holding something in his hands. What is it? A long branch. No, a rope. The rope that is dragging me forward. It's tied under my arms. I must have been dreaming, because I remember falling into the water. There were lots of people on shore throwing stones at me. If even one of them struck me, I would drown. Stones rained down all around me, but none of them hit me. I was able to walk on water. Then I saw a gray body underneath me. It was racing through the water at great speed. I couldn't see what it was. But now I have awakened from the dream. I am lying here throwing up on myself. It's not sour, stinking vomit, just water. I am lying on the snow and looking up at the stars overhead. I hear somebody talking. He seems in a frenzy.

I can't feel my arms or my legs. Not my face either. Only the ax that has grown onto my hand. I try to say something, but nothing comes out. I don't recognize myself. Am I a dead man who's been hauled up out of the water? From the blue ice down below? Is that why I'm so cold? Somebody rescued me. A big black crab wearing a hat. Now I hear his footsteps on the hard-packed snow. He comes close. Says something. Repeats it. I think he's asking me a question. But it can't be English. Now I see him. He has on a black hat with a round brim. Under the hat he's wearing some kind of scarf tied around his head, covering his ears. His face is as dark as an otter's. He squats down. I close my eyes. Then I feel a hand on my forehead. He is stroking my skin. My mother is the only one who has ever stroked my forehead before. It's a warm hand. He unbuttons my jacket. I can't move. He sticks his hand inside my clothes and places it on my chest. And leaves it there. Then he says something again, but I can't understand him. I've heard English spoken every day for weeks. I should be able to recognize that language, even though I can't speak it myself. No, this isn't English.

I open my eyes and look up at the face above me. He isn't going to hurt me, is he? But didn't he just rescue me? Yes, that's why I'm lying here and not at the bottom of the lake. It's as if I've come ashore once again. I was way up there in the sky. A star. I thought I was dead, and he has brought me back to life. I've heard the gypsies can do that sort of thing. And I think this man must be a gypsy. Now he's nodding and muttering something. The brim of his hat is blocking out the moonlight. His face is in shadow. He's still holding his hand on my chest. It's the warmest hand I've ever felt.

I can feel myself breathing again. And it hurts. A rib, I remember now. I fell into a creek. No, I jumped over it. I can move my head now. Take a look around. The enormous lake. The ice-covered bay. The hole in the ice. The moon. The black water merging with the sky, like the sea. And behind the gypsy a cross. Two sticks lashed together with rope. That was what I saw just before I went under. He is patting my chest. Gives a toss of his head. Does he want me to go with him? He puts his hand to his cheek, as if to signal that he's tired. Does he want me to go with him and sleep? But I need

*to find Knut's boat shed. From there it's a straight path up
to his cabin.*

*I try to sit up but can only manage to move my hands a bit.
So how will I be able to find my way to Knut and Nanette?
It's impossible. Either I lie here all alone and freeze to death,
or I go with the man who rescued me. Because that is what
he did. He rescued me from the water. Brought me down
from the stars. I try to nod, but can't manage it. He seems
to understand. He grabs the rope and again starts dragging me across the packed snow. It's worse here than out on
the ice. There are rocks and tussocks under the snow. The
ground goes up and down. But he's careful. He drags me in
between the big pine trees. I can hear a river. It must be the
same one I saw just before I fell through the ice. Where are
we going? But anything is better than lying there alone and
freezing to death next to that cross, even though pain shoots
through me when I slide over a tussock or a rock.*

*I don't let go of the ax. The gypsy drags me and the ax over
the snow. Up above, between the big pines, I can see the
moon. It has followed me the whole way. I was up there
with it, but now I'm back on earth, where I belong. He stops.
I turn my head and see a sort of sod hut like the Lapps
build. He says something in his gypsy language, comes
over to me, squats down, unties the rope and takes it off
me. Then he grabs me under the arms and lifts me up.
Sets me on my feet. I'm still holding the ax. I don't think
I could let it go even if I wanted to. I try to stand on my
own, but I can't. He grabs me as I fall. Then he partially
carries me, partially supports me over to the hut. It's not
like an ordinary sod hut. It's covered with birch bark. Ani-*

mal hides are hanging from poles that are stuck between the trees. This place smells of animals. He moves aside a big sheet of birch bark. That must be the door. I fall into the dark.

IT WAS SO QUIET Lance heard a ringing in his ears. He was sitting on post. Andy was supposed to start at the river and head west, crossing the path of the two first drives. Along a creek bed they thought would be promising. Lance was positioned near a small area that had been clear cut, half hidden behind a tree. The clearing was covered with a thick underbrush of raspberry bushes, but they weren't so tall that they'd block a deer from view. There were also a number of tall, slender aspens, as well as some bigger birch trees.

Lance was annoyed to feel his big stomach pressing against his thighs. Actually, it disgusted him. He thought about how easily Andy moved through the woods. No matter how much he ate, he kept the same lean physique. Tammy and Chrissy too. They were a thin family.

He and Andy had exchanged only a few words, and only about the hunt, after Lance had mentioned Chrissy. Neither of them said any more than was necessary. He just hoped Andy also wanted to get this whole expedition over with as soon as possible. That he wasn't trying to pull something behind his back. But it was obvious Andy was feeling uneasy. He could tell his brother knew something.

Lance pictured the body of Georg Lofthus the way it had looked when he found the dead man on that morning nearly four months ago. He couldn't even imagine what emotions must have provoked such a brutal attack. For a moment he thought about the cat hissing in the dark. How he'd struck blow after blow, and kept at it long after the cat had fallen silent. But good Lord, it was a cat! And one that was seriously injured. He hadn't had the heart to just drive away and leave the poor animal like that.

Andy would never hurt me, he thought. Not even if I turned him in. And yet Lance wasn't so sure about that. Because if he did turn Andy in, his brother would spend the rest of his life behind bars, cut off from his family, locked up with hardened criminals. Lance assumed he'd go to great lengths to avoid ending up like that. But how far would he go?

Lance was keeping an eye on the clearing the whole time. This took some effort since nothing was happening out there, but a good hunter had to master the art of constant vigilance, or else he wouldn't have a chance when something finally did happen. That was something he fully understood. Now it occurred to him that this might also be the right way to deal with his brother. Stay alert the whole time, even now, when nothing seemed to be happening. Especially now. If he didn't, all of a sudden it might be too late.

I'm not taking any chances, he thought.

It had started to drizzle. The same dismal cold rain. He raised his hands to his lips to blow on his fingers. He never wore mittens or gloves while out hunting. And it wasn't just because he needed to pull the trigger. He could have done like so many other hunters did, cutting off the index finger on their right glove or wearing fingerless mitts. For Lance it was a matter of his *grip* on the rifle and having complete contact between the palms of his hands and the stock of the gun, whether it was made of wood or, as in his case, fiberglass. He rubbed his hands hard against each other until they turned a fiery red. Then he picked up his rifle and resumed the same motionless position.

What if Andy had lost control, just like that time in

the school yard long ago? If it comes down to him or me, thought Lance, how far am *I* willing to go?

ANDY WAS WALKING ALONG A CREEK, holding his rifle in his hands. All around him grew tall maple trees. They were spaced relatively far apart, which gave the woods a more open, almost park-like feel—something that was quite unusual for the area. When he reached a place where the creek made a ninety-degree turn, he stopped and looked around. A couple of rocks were sticking up out of the foaming white water. All the rain over the past few weeks had made for a forceful current. Even so, he leaped from the bank and crossed the creek with a couple of light, quick steps, almost as if he were dancing across the rocks, holding his gun in his right hand, his left arm outstretched to keep his balance. He disappeared among some bushes on the opposite bank, but soon reemerged.

Suddenly Andy spun around and stared straight ahead. Lance swiftly pulled back behind the small spruce tree. But when he ventured another look, he saw that his brother was continuing along the creek at the same slow pace. It didn't look like he'd noticed anything, but if he had, it would have been nothing more than a split second of movement. It was probably coincidence that he had spun around to look in his brother's direction.

Now Lance left his hiding place and walked along the ridge, making sure the whole time that he couldn't be seen from the creek bed below. As long as he stayed up here, it shouldn't be a problem to reach the post before Andy did. The distance he needed to cover was significantly shorter than the route his brother was taking. He could cut straight across the ridge and he'd be at his post. Andy, on the other hand, had to follow the creek, which meandered in a great loop around the same ridge. It was in this valley that they were hoping to find deer.

The backs of Lance's hands were burning from the cold. The light drizzle continued to come down. Little more than a fine mist, and it wasn't going to get any worse. It didn't bother him that he could no longer see his brother. Andy would have to stay down in the valley if he was going to carry out the drive properly. Lance felt he now had him under control. It was only a matter of waiting for a while; then Andy would once again appear among the big maple trees below.

It occurred to Lance that he'd never been in exactly this spot before. It was true that he and Andy had hunted in this area several times, and as part of his job, he'd driven along a gravel road on the north side of the ridge. When he was a kid he'd also played fur trapper out here with his cousin Gary Hansen. Yet in all these years he'd never come up onto the ridge itself.

It was like a plateau, fairly flat and good for walking, mostly covered with a sparse conifer forest. He could see the lake and Highway 61. The cars looked like little matchboxes. Because of the distance, they all seemed to be moving at a snail's pace. For a moment he almost forgot why he was here. He remembered that time when they'd stood and looked at the lake in the dark, with the reflection of the moonlight spreading over the whole, huge surface of the water. The world around them cloaked in darkness. Was it *here* we stood? he wondered. Had he been here before, after all? He knew that couldn't be true; they'd been much farther away from the lake back then. Not a single light had been visible, not from any houses or cars. What if Dad could see us now? he thought. He was the one who taught us to appreciate all this.

In his mind Lance pictured his brother holding out

his hand and shouting: *"Come on and eat, and be quick about it, you fucking ungrateful little birds!"* It was a grotesque parody of the way his father used to talk, made even more grotesque because the object of ridicule was deceased. The dead should be respected, he thought. Nobody knows what it means to be dead. Nobody knows where the dead are.

Now he saw Andy again. He'd covered a good distance, but it should still be no problem to reach the post before he did. Lance had the situation under control. He followed his brother, making sure the whole time that he'd be able to make a quick retreat and slip out of sight. For that reason he kept a suitable distance away from the edge of the ridge so that all he really needed to do was duck down to avoid being seen from the valley floor.

Andy stopped and stood still next to a big boulder. He seemed to be looking at something on the ground. Then Lance realized what his brother was doing. With a slight feeling of discomfort he pulled the rifle strap off his shoulder and raised the gun, as if he were about to shoot. When he looked through the scope, the trees in the valley came into sharp focus. He had to move the scope back and forth a bit before he found Andy, who was pissing against the big boulder. Like a dog, thought Lance. Steam rose up from the urine. He made a point of keeping the crosshairs off Andy. For a second they settled on the boulder, which was about three feet from his brother's left shoulder. The whole time Lance was keenly aware of the placement of the fingers of his right hand. Not because he was afraid of shooting his brother by accident, but there was something frightening about looking at him in this way. There was a certain tension about standing here like this, even though he wasn't aiming at Andy, because he wasn't. He was just studying him. But he'd stood in this same position so many times, aiming at a deer. If a deer had been standing there right now, taking a piss, he would have shot it.

Andy finished and pulled up his rain pants. Then he started walking again. Viewed through the rifle scope, he seemed wrapped in total silence. As if he were moving through a different world than the one in which Lance found himself. When he lowered his gun, Andy was instantly far away, as were any sounds he made.

Lance headed through the pine trees, holding his rifle in his right hand. If a deer appeared, he was going to shoot it, no matter what Andy might think about why he was up on the ridge. He could say the deer had first turned up near the post but took off as soon as he raised his gun, and so he'd followed the animal up here. It wasn't really important whether Andy believed the story or not. The only thing that mattered was bringing this hunting expedition to an end.

Couldn't he just call it quits? A tempting idea, but it wasn't that simple. Lance couldn't think of anything that would make his brother more suspicious than if he phoned to say he was giving up. In the twenty-six years they'd been doing this, they had never once called off a hunt. And even though he might have convinced Andy that he'd suddenly taken ill, doing so would merely postpone things. He couldn't very well keep playing sick for the rest of November. Sooner or later they'd have to set out again to finish what they'd started today. There was only one way out of this, and that was for one of them to bag a deer. That would finally put an end to it. With a whole year until next time, he'd be able to think up some excuse for never going out hunting again.

He could no longer see Andy, but he spied an open area at the bottom of the valley, and his brother couldn't possibly have reached that spot yet. All Lance had to do was wait a few minutes, and then he'd have him in sight again. He couldn't see the lake or the road anymore, just the valley below, and on the other side the terrain rose up to approximately the same height as the ridge where he was standing. He leaned against the trunk of a pine, focusing his gaze on the open area below.

As he stood there, he began to freeze. The cold moved up his legs to his hips and the small of his back. It crept farther up, until even his scalp was shivering. His jaw muscles began to tremble. He had to stand still and wait for Andy to appear in the clearing down in the valley; he couldn't lose him now. He couldn't allow himself to jump up and down or do a few knee bends. It was essential that he remained as still as possible. That was why he stood there, soundlessly shaking, with his back pressed against a pine tree. It felt like the last remnants of warmth, a sort of core somewhere deep inside his body, was being pushed out by the cold.

Just like seven years ago, when he'd dreamed for the last time. He was standing at the deepest spot in Lake Superior. If he'd stood there in reality, it would have been 1,332 feet below the surface. A blue-shimmering landscape all around him. Icebergs reaching up like sharp peaks in a mountain chain, each one higher than the last. It was the most beautiful thing he'd ever seen. But the marrow in his bones had started turning to an icy slush. If the dream had continued, there would have been nothing more than a skeleton of ice left of him. And in the form of that ice skeleton, he would have kept on moving around at the bottom of the lake. He pictured a skeleton, shiny with frost, plodding along. He heard the sound it made, like the most delicate of chimes. I never would have woken up from that, he thought. I would have died in bed. Ever since that time, he'd had the feeling this cold place was waiting for him. That it was still there. He just didn't know in which world.

Andy hadn't yet appeared below. Anyone who wanted

to pass through the valley would have to make a great effort *not* to cross that open plain. The only other option was to cross the ridge itself, to climb up the steep slope and come up here. But why would Andy do something like that? In terms of the hunt, it would be utterly pointless. It was down on the valley floor, in the stands of maple trees, that the deer would be found. The buck would most likely continue along the valley when it noticed the driver coming from behind. Up here, on the other hand, it would be impossible to predict which way an animal would head. There was nothing about the landscape on the ridge that pointed in any specific direction, as it did in the valley. If Andy chose to come straight over the ridge, that decision would have nothing to do with any deer.

Lance was still leaning against the pine. He was freezing. The external cold stinging his hands and face was one thing. It had also crept under the layers of clothes he was wearing and turned the skin on his thighs numb. This was the sort of cold he was used to, since he'd grown up in Duluth, after all. Cold that stung your skin was no cause for concern. It was the cold that seemed to be coming from inside him that was worse. It didn't cause any clear, tangible pain, but it had seized hold of his guts and organs, as if the cold hand of a giant had grabbed him from inside.

He started walking as fast as he could toward the post near the small logged area. His body soon warmed up, and a light film of sweat appeared on his forehead. Now he just had to get there before Andy. But what if his brother was already on his way across the ridge? Maybe they were actually very close to each other. Lance paused for a moment to listen, but he realized instantly that it was pointless. If his brother could sneak up on a deer and shoot the animal, as he'd done so many times before, it would take a stroke of luck for Lance to hear him.

It was hard going through the tall heath, but even though he quickly tired, there was no way he could stop to rest. First, because he had to reach the post before Andy did. And second, because he was afraid he'd start freezing again if he stopped. The air was definitely colder than only a few minutes ago. It was no longer raining. He huffed and puffed as he made his way through the pine forest at the top of the ridge. There wasn't a deer in the world that wouldn't have heard him coming from far off. Suddenly this whole thing seemed stupid and degrading. He was a grown man who had gone out hunting since he was thirteen years old. And a forest cop, on top of it. Yet he was carrying on like this. He should have stayed calmly in position, with all his attention focused on waiting for a deer. A big buck might have passed the post while he was out spying on his brother as he took a leak.

It didn't take long for Lance to cross the ridge. Fortunately, Andy was nowhere in sight when he reached the post. He took up position, partially hidden behind the same shaggy spruce tree as before, and tried to get control of his breathing.

By now it seemed unlikely they'd do any more hunting even though they hadn't shot any deer on this drive either. Lance felt like the whole way of life he was familiar with was coming to an end, and he couldn't even imagine what would happen after today's hunt. Couldn't imagine anything "after the hunt" at all. For a moment he pictured Andy as he'd seen him in the scope of his rifle a short time ago. He now felt there was something irreparable about that moment, that he'd crossed a line, and it would be impossible to cross back over. Aiming at a human being was practically a crime. Even though he'd been very careful not to let the crosshairs touch the figure of his own brother, he'd stood there with his rifle raised and studied Andy through the scope. In all the years they'd gone hunting together, he'd never done anything like that before; the thought had never even occurred to him. And if it had, he would have certainly felt horrified. But that was no longer true.

Lance raised his gun into firing position a couple of times, just to make sure he still had it in him. He wasn't entirely convinced he would get into proper position, but of course he did. He'd handled a rifle since he was eight and gone out hunting from the age of thirteen. He went on his first deer-hunting expedition with his brother as a twenty-year-old. He wasn't particularly interested in guns, but he liked the focus and the precision a perfect shot demanded. The correct line between his eye, the scope, and the target. Ever since his father first taught him to shoot with an air gun, he'd enjoyed hunting and felt it was something he was good at. But not once in all that time, at least as far as he could remember, had he ever raised his rifle to his shoulder because he was uncertain about whether he still had it in him.

Andy had not crossed the open plain at the bottom of the valley. At least not while Lance was watching. What if he'd gone straight over the ridge and was on his way here from behind? The post was at the base of the slope, and the terrain rose up steeply behind him. There were a lot of trees up there, relatively speaking, mostly aspen and birch, but it wouldn't be impossible to find a spot, maybe fifty yards away, with a clear sight down to him. Lance turned halfway so that he could alternately keep an eye on the clear-cut and the slope. The temperature must have dropped below freezing, because now the leaves were crunching under his boots. That would make it more difficult for Andy to sneak up on a deer, but also easier for Lance to hear him. He listened for the snapping of a twig, the crackling of almost-frozen leaves, but he heard nothing.

The cold had begun to seep inside him again. A faint trembling was spreading through his torso, his breath was white with frost. He felt an urge to jump up and down or to flap his arms, but it would be best if he didn't make a sound. He was just going to have to let the cold eat into him.

Again he raised the rifle into firing position. He was still able to manage it just fine, but he had no idea how much longer he could do it. Soon the cold inside his body would start to hamper his movements. That's when the deer will show up, he thought. When I'm no longer capable of taking a precise shot. That's when it will suddenly be standing right there. Either the deer, or Andy. His brother would appear when Lance could no longer defend himself. Yet he was also the only one who could release him from the cold. As soon as Andy turned up, Lance would be free to move about as much as he liked. Until then, he was at the mercy of the cold, which was penetrating ever deeper inside him. If I stand here long enough, I'll freeze into ice, he thought. Just like at the bottom of the lake. And it's 1,332 feet up to the surface.

HE JUST BARELY REGISTERED the vibrations against his numb thigh. He opened the pocket flap and took out his cell phone. It was Andy's number on the display.

"Yep?" he said, but his voice was almost inaudible. He cleared his throat and tried again. "Hello?"

"I'm right below you," said his brother.

"Good."

"See anything?"

"Nothing. Did you?"

"Nothing," said Andy.

"Hmm . . ."

"Well, I'll be there in a sec." Andy broke the connection before Lance could say anything more.

Lance leaned his rifle against a tree trunk and began flapping his arms. His brother soon emerged from the edge of the woods.

"Are you cold?" asked Andy when he came closer.

"Naw."

Lance slung his rifle over his shoulder. They avoided looking each other in the eye.

"So you didn't see anything?" he asked.

"No deer, in any case."

"Something else?" said Lance.

"I don't know . . ."

"What?"

"I saw a man," said Andy.

"A man? Where?"

His brother looked at him. Lance thought he held his gaze a little too long, and finally he had to look away.

"Up on the ridge."

"Well, at least he won't cause any trouble up there."

Andy looked like he wanted to say something more. He cleared his throat a few times and seemed about to speak. Instead he turned around, lifted his Minnesota Twins cap, and scratched his scalp. Then he put the cap back on.

"Not a single deer," he said with his back turned to Lance.

"What should we do now?"

"Keep going," said Andy.

"But where?"

Andy turned back to face him. "Between the highway and the lake. We're allowed to do that, right?"

Lance wondered if he should lie, but that would just mean they'd have to go out again next weekend. They might as well be done with it now.

"Uh-huh. Our licenses include the area along the lake between the Temperance River and the Cross River."

"I'm sure there's gotta be some deer down there," said Andy.

"But there's also a greater risk we'll run into tourists."

"No, the weather's too lousy. I think we'll have the woods to ourselves. But first let's eat. I'm hungry."

THEY REACHED THE PARKING LOT near the Cross River without exchanging a word during the half hour it took them to get there. Lance went over to his Jeep and opened the tailgate. While he was wrapping his rifle in the brown blanket, he heard his brother's voice right behind him.

"What the hell have you been doing?"

He tried to turn around, but it was difficult since he was bending forward into the vehicle. Andy reached in next to him and grabbed the wrench. Lance had forgotten it was underneath the blanket.

"Oh, that," he said.

"Did you kill somebody, or what?"

Lance backed out of the Jeep and straightened up.

"Yes," he said.

Andy laughed nervously.

"I ran over a cat last night. Had to kill it."

"On your way home after hunting?"

"No, later on. Up near Reservation River. Didn't even see it before I hit it."

"Why were you up there yesterday?"

"Visiting Willy."

"Willy?"

"Dupree."

"Oh."

I don't think he's a gypsy, this man sitting wrapped up in a blanket and humming over there in the corner. He's an Indian. In the light from the fire that's burning between us, I see things no gypsy would travel around with. I can't even guess what those things might be. One looks like a small snowshoe, no bigger than my hand. Several big feathers are hanging from it. White feathers with black tips. I must have swallowed a lump of ice, and it's not melting, just spreading cold through my body. I can't feel the heat from the fire at all. I just see the light. I think I might be dying, but that doesn't seem to matter anymore. I can't remember if there was something important I needed to do first. Don't think so. I wouldn't mind dying now, if it's like when I was in the lake. Down there, at least, I wasn't cold. And there were stars and the moon and blue mountains. The ax went with me into the water and came back up with me again. I can barely feel the handle in my hand, but it's still there.

The man over there is moving. I hear something clattering, like a cooking pot. He crawls on his knees over to the door and pushes aside the big piece of birch bark. He wears the round-brimmed black hat indoors too. Underneath the hat he has on a scarf. I can hear him scratching in the snow with something. Oh, I think he's filling the pot with snow. Then he backs in through the door and closes it up again. He hangs the pot over the fire. Is he making soup? Pea soup with chunks of pork? Not even that would thaw the ice inside me. That's how cold I am. He sits down in the corner again. Pulls his knees up to his chin, wraps the blanket around himself, and settles down like before. There is some sort of picture on the blanket, but I can't see what it is. There seem to be strong colors too. Red and white, I think, but there's not enough light in here for me to be sure.

Now he's starting to hum again. Is it some sort of song? He rocks back and forth. I don't like it. But they don't eat people here, do they? I've never heard that Indians eat people. Maybe they did before the white folks came here, but not anymore. My lips feel like they've been flayed raw. My mouth froze to the packed snow, and I've broken a rib. I'm shaking all over. Only my right hand refuses to move. It's clamped like the claws of an eagle around the ax handle. But the rest of me is shaking so hard I can barely see. I think even my eyes are shaking in their sockets. My teeth are chattering. I catch a glimpse of the Indian above me. He bends down closer, but I'm shaking so bad I can't see his face. It's nothing but a dark patch.

I don't understand what he's saying. I can't tell whether it's English or an Indian language. I think he sounds scared. Or maybe angry. I try to say something, but all I hear is the chattering of my own teeth. He puts his hand on my forehead and mutters something. His hand is ice cold now. Even colder than I am inside. I'm freezing inside and out. When the cold outside meets the cold inside me, I will die. I think that's how it will happen. Because then there won't be any warmth anywhere. Even the fire seems cold now. It's glowing, but it gives off no heat. It's glowing in the middle of the darkest forest. In the middle of the night. The forest animals stay away from the fire. They fear it, just as we fear the Lord. "Thou shalt have no other gods before me. That is, above all else we shall fear and love God and put our trust in Him. There is only one true God, the Creator and Lord of all things. The heathens' gods are dead idols." They are hollow tree stumps. If you kick them, rats and toads come out. That's what their gods are: rats and toads and snakes. The Almighty Lord is in heaven, but these unhappy souls have never heard of him. Or of Jesus Christ. The man sitting over there doesn't know who Jesus is. He offers young goats and lambs to Baal.

But I have almost been in heaven. I'll be going back there soon. Up into the vault of the sky, and through it, beyond to God's Kingdom, where its radiance will warm me again. There it might take two years before I have enough money for my own boat. If you're not afraid of hard work, of course. And there's so much fish that you can earn more in a week than a man does in a whole year back home. That's why I have to go there, to earn money. I want to have my own boat and my own house. I want to eat pea soup with pork. He has taken the pot off the fire. He's crumbling something into the water. I don't know what it is. It looks like a piece of bark. The whole time he keeps up that cursed humming. As if he's singing something into me. I don't like it. Maybe it's idol worship. And now he sticks his hand under his blanket and takes something out. It looks like a small pouch. He sticks his fingers down into it and then sprinkles a pinch of something into the pot. He's probably not making pea soup. It's a witch's brew. And he wants me to drink it.

"I believe in God, the Father Almighty, maker of heaven and earth. And in Jesus Christ, his only son, our Lord, who was conceived by the Holy Spirit, born of the Virgin Mary, suffered under Pontius Pilate, was crucified, died, and was buried. He descended into hell. On the third day He rose again from the dead. He ascended into heaven, and sits at the right hand of God the Father Almighty. From thence He will come to judge the living and the dead." So he will return

here to earth, to judge us all, whether we are alive or dead. But where on this earth will he find the dead? Will Jesus open the graves? Every single grave in every single cemetery in the whole world? Won't they come out as skeletons and half-rotten carcasses? Is that what will happen? If so, a terrible stench will spread over the day of resurrection. And it won't be a pleasant sight either. There must be many more dead than people who are alive. What will they all do? Maybe the same things they did when they were still alive. The dead baker will set about baking again, and all the fishing boats will be rowed by skeletons wearing oilskin hats. That seems very unlikely, even though it says as much in the catechism. The classrooms will be filled with skeleton children. No matter where you go, you will meet the dead.

But surely that's not the way it will happen. There must be more than a sudden mass ascension to heaven for both the dead and the living. Well, at least for those who have been God's obedient children. The others, the sinners, will plunge straight down into the blazing embers, where they will burn for all eternity. And I suppose that afterward the earth will be empty. Or maybe the animals will remain. Because animals and fish cannot be judged, can they? So there will probably be good fishing, but no one left to fish. The heathens live in hell here on earth. That's what I've heard. It's because they are living without the grace of God. The man sitting over there in the corner is without grace. But I have grace. That's why I'm no longer freezing. Because now I feel nothing. Not the cold, not the heat. Maybe that means I'm about to die. But what does it matter? Won't I just rise up again? Up to the moon and the stars? Yes, and then beyond them, to enter the Kingdom of Heaven on the other side.

But there was something important I was supposed to do first. And now I remember what I'm doing here. I'm only a couple of hours away from the log cabin that belongs to Knut. And I'm very good at hiking. But then I fell through the ice. I have not been up in the vault of the sky. That was just something I imagined. I almost drowned. I was practically dead when the heathen rescued me. Because that's what he did. And because of that, I don't know whether I need to be scared of him or not. But I will never drink that witch's brew of his, if that's what he wants. It's un-Christian, what he put in the water. I have such a yearning for pea soup with pieces of pork, but I refuse to think about everybody back home. When I get to Knut and Nanette's cabin, they'll probably give me porridge and coffee. And that will taste good, even though pea soup with pork would be much better. If I don't get warm inside soon, I'm going to die. I make an attempt to sit up, but when I manage it, I see that I'm naked. The fur rug slipped down when I sat up. I didn't even know I was lying under a fur. I thought I was just stretched out with my clothes on. But I'm naked to the waist. The fur is covering the rest of me. Did I take off my clothes? Did the Indian take off my clothes? When did that happen? Did I fall asleep?

I lift the fur rug and peer underneath. My God! I'm completely naked. Now I'm never going to reach my uncle's place. I can't walk naked through the woods or I'll freeze to death. But where are my clothes? I can't go searching for them, not naked as I am. Then the man comes over to me and places his hands on me. One hand on each shoulder. I try to resist, but he presses me back down to the ground, as if I were a child. I have almost no strength. All I can do is stay lying here until he gives me my clothes back. I have to trust that he'll give them back. Because he's just trying to help me, isn't he? If it weren't for him, I'd be dead.

He's talking to me. I think it's English, but I don't understand a word. His face looks filthy with grease and soot from the fire. He's holding me down just by pointing at me. Without even touching me. I can't get past that finger of his. It's impossible to move it aside. It's the darkest finger I've ever seen. He keeps on pointing as he uses his other hand to search for something. Now I feel how cold it is in here. The cold is biting into my naked skin. The Indian has found what he was looking for. Again he bends over me. In his hand he's holding something that looks like a bunch of straw or hay. That's right, it's dried grass, I can feel it now. He presses it against my chest and starts rubbing very hard and fast. The only thing that happens is that I feel even colder. I'm shaking all over. My body rises in an arch, with only the back of my head and the heels of my feet on the ground. I turn to ice. Soon I'll shatter into a thousand pieces. But he just keeps rubbing harder and faster, and the surface of my skin starts to warm up. My body is not arched, after all. I'm lying on my back just like before. The Indian has pulled down the fur rug and is rubbing my thighs. I can't manage to lift even a finger. I just lie there naked under the heathen's hand. Surely it must be a sin, what he's doing. And I'm lying here with everything exposed. But he pretends not to see it. Rubs the bunch of hay hard and fast along my thigh. I notice a prickling and stinging sensation. And now he continues down my legs. My calves and feet. Rubs me all the way down to my toes. And under my feet.

Then he starts on my chest and shoulders again. My arms still feel cold. But now he starts working on them, and they begin to prickle and sting too. His expression is solemn. I feel a warm gust of air blowing over my naked hips. It's heat from the fire.

5

ANDY SCREWED THE CAP BACK ON and put the milk bottle inside the backpack, which was propped between his feet. He blew on his coffee and cautiously took a sip before setting the cup in the holder between the seats.

They had driven down to the other parking area, the closest one to Baraga's Cross. Now they were both sitting in Lance's Jeep. The temperature was starting to feel more comfortable with the engine idling. They had parked with their backs to the lake. From where they were sitting, they could see along Baraga Cross Road, which led up to Highway 61. About four months ago Lance had stood here with Sheriff Bill Eggum and the two police officers Sparky Redmeyer and Mike Jones, speculating about whether the murder of the Norwegian tourist was the first homicide to occur in Cook County.

That was when the link between Swamper Caribou's disappearance and the murder of the Norwegian canoeist Georg Lofthus had come about—when Lance decided to find out if there had ever been a murder committed here in the past. He was the one who made the connection, because he was the only one who knew the truth about the two cases. Not to mention that in both instances the murder had been committed by someone in his own family. If it was true Swamper Caribou had been killed, that is.

Lance took a few sips of coffee and set his cup back in the holder, next to his brother's. He still had the feeling there would be no "after the hunt." Not even another drive. Because what were they supposed to do? If they shot a deer, would they then head home to Lance's place and cut up the carcass the way they usually did? With dried blood on their hands? What would they say to each other? Or, if this drive also proved fruitless, would they stand next to their vehicles and talk a bit morosely about how strange it was not to have shot a deer? Then agree to try again the following weekend? He didn't think any of this seemed likely. He felt that it couldn't possibly happen. It was like watching a movie he'd seen many times before and trying to imagine that this time the ending would be different. Yet he knew there was only one ending to the movie. It was impossible to believe the story would suddenly change. And it was just as impossible for Lance to picture an ending to this day. Any end at all.

"So, how shall we do it?" Was there something threatening about Andy's voice?

"Do what?"

"You want to do the drive this time?"

"Sure. All right," replied Lance.

"In which direction?"

"I don't know . . . Is there any wind to speak of?"

"A few gusts here and there, but it's impossible to predict where they're coming from."

"So where do you want to take up the post?"

"Somewhere near here. The terrain is more rugged over by the Temperance."

"But it's really dense birch forest."

"Yeah, but there's a clear stretch along the shore. I can stand over there."

"That's close to . . ."

"Does it matter?" Andy took a gulp of coffee.

"No."

The crime scene was a couple of hundred yards inside the birch forest. The young Norwegian had been found lying on the ground, naked and with his head bashed in. Flies had flown into Lance's mouth as he stood over the body. Afterward, when he was in the parking lot with Sheriff Eggum and his men, he'd had a strange feeling that both the site and the dead man somehow belonged to him, and that every time someone took a picture of the corpse or jotted down something in a notebook, they were taking something away from him personally. He paused to mull this over, but he no longer had that same feeling. Now he thought about the crime scene as a place he had no desire to revisit. A *cold* place. Above all, cold. Even though it had been hot when he stood there in the summer. He clearly remembered how the drops of sweat had run into his eyes.

It was the last place he ever wanted to set foot again, but would he even recognize the spot amid all those stunted birch trees? Except for the fact that it was the setting where he'd found the dead man, there was nothing special about the place. By now all traces of the crime would have long since vanished, and without them, it would be difficult to find the precise location. Yet Lance thought he'd sense it if he accidentally found himself at that same spot. How could he not? It was there that he first came into contact with what would change everything he'd ever known. He imagined that he'd notice it because of a sudden drop in temperature. As if he were stepping inside a small, isolated pocket of cold.

"Sure?" said Andy.

"Yeah."

"So you'll drive the Jeep over to the Temperance and park there, okay?"

"Uh-huh."

"Then wait fifteen minutes before you start the drive."

"Fine," said Lance.

He bit into his sandwich. It had dried out, and the food seemed to swell in his mouth as he chewed. Finally he had to force himself to swallow the big lump of bread, which hurt as it slid down his esophagus.

"Mind if I turn on the radio?" he asked.

"Go ahead," replied Andy.

The radio was tuned to Minnesota Public Radio, as usual. It was the program *Wait Wait . . . Don't Tell Me!*—an informal contest in which the listeners and a panel of guests in the studio tested their knowledge about the news stories of the past week.

"Which song was chosen the 'saddest love song of all time' by NPR's listeners?" asked the moderator.

Lance switched off the radio.

"Do you know the answer?" he asked.

Andy didn't reply, just sat and stared out the side window.

"The saddest love song of all time?" Lance repeated.

"Have you ever gone swimming in the lake?" asked Andy without turning around.

"In the lake? No, I don't think so."

"Me neither. Isn't that strange?"

"The water never gets warm enough."

"But still," said Andy. "Think of all the other places we've gone swimming. In small lakes and rivers. But never in the big lake that's been right in front of us the whole time."

Lance turned the radio back on, but they were done with the saddest love song of all time. Now they'd turned to politics. Something about proposed legislation in the Senate. He switched it off again.

"I think maybe it's because the lake is so big," said Andy. "When you live your whole life next to something that big . . ."

"Yeah?"

"Well . . . in the end you don't really *see* it anymore."

"No, it's because of the temperature of the water," Lance said. "It's as cold as ice."

He thought about the lake beneath the moon, on that night long ago. How many times had he seen Lake Superior in the moonlight? Hundreds of times, no doubt. Then what was so special about that particular memory? Of course it happened to be an early memory—he couldn't have been more than ten at the time—but that wasn't what made it special. Nor the fact that all three of them had been there together, because that wasn't so unusual, especially in the woods or out in the fields. No, the memory must have simply risen up from the deep, so to speak, where it had lain dormant and unnoticed for years, presumably ever since his childhood. Suddenly he had recalled how they stood there together, looking at the lake off in the distance. A huge, metallic, shimmering surface under the moon. Endless. And that was what Dad wanted, he thought now. He wanted us to remember it sometime in the future, when we needed it. That was why he took us there. But the memory hadn't come back to Lance until today. So it must be today that he needed to remember it. Inside the dark tunnel where he and Andy were the only living things.

Andy said something, barely audible over the sound of his lips moving and his breathing, as if thoughts were leaking out of his mouth without him noticing.

"What did you say?" asked Lance.

"Huh?"

"You said something."

"Unh-uh."

"Yes, you did."

"No, I didn't."

Lance took another bite of his dry sandwich. Drank some coffee.

"Do you remember Debbie? The girl I dated a long time ago?"

"Don't think so."

"Debbie Ahonen, from the town of Finland? Twenty years ago."

"Oh. Vaguely."

"She moved to California with a policeman from . . . somewhere or other. I met her again this past summer. She got divorced and moved back here."

"Huh."

"Now she's living with Richie Akkola."

"Old Richie who owns the grocery store?"

"And the gas station."

"But he's gotta be—"

"At least seventy. I know. Debbie's mother is sick, and Akkola's been helping them out financially."

"Are you saying that . . . that she . . . ?"

"There you have the saddest love song of all time," said Lance.

"If that's what you think, then you don't know much about love."

He'd never heard Andy talk that way before. There was something unnatural about it. His brother had already turned his face away and was again looking out the side window. Was it the lake he was staring at? Lance would have to roll down his window and stick out his head if he wanted to see the lake. Although he could see it in the rearview mirror, but only a thin sliver of the water. As was so often the case, the lake looked gray and cold. He thought about what Andy had just said, about swimming in Lake Superior. Who the hell would ask a question like that? *Have you ever gone swimming in the lake?* That was something only tourists did. North Shore folks *drowned* in the lake, if they didn't dream of walking on the bottom of it. With 1,332 feet up to the surface. Bones of ice. That's the stuff we're made of, he thought. That was what his father had once said when they were talking about Thormod Olson who fell through the ice and survived a night in the woods in wet clothes and with the temperature way below freezing. *That's the stuff we're made of.*

Andy hadn't moved. He was sitting there in silence with his face turned away. Lance didn't know what to say. He thought the word *love* was still hovering inside the car. Of all the things his brother might have said, it was the word *love* that made it so difficult for Lance to say anything else.

"Well," he said. "I guess we should . . ."

Andy didn't reply.

Lance stuffed the last of his sandwich in his mouth and proceeded to chew. He had a feeling it was important to refuel.

"But that's how it's always been," said Andy.

"What do you mean?" asked Lance, his mouth full.

"What you said about the lake. You've always thought you know more than anybody else, but the truth is you know *less*. At least about things that matter."

Lance was just about to tell him to shut up, but he changed his mind. Maybe it would be smart to see where this led. He deliberately stared straight ahead and didn't say a word.

Andy let the silence go on for a while. Then he said, "All that history stuff, for instance . . . You seem to think it makes you a big shot, or something. But the truth is that people are *laughing* at you, Lance. That's why you never hear anything worthwhile—because nobody tells you anything. They laugh at you instead."

"Why are you telling me this?"

"Because you should know . . . that you're trampling around in people's lives without paying any attention to them. Without even realizing what you're doing. That's the sort of thing you just don't seem to get. You don't see who people really are. Or what's really going on."

"So what's really going on?"

Andy turned and looked Lance in the eye. "People are living their own lives," he said. "That's what's going on. And it's none of your business. You have no right to go trampling . . . to go stomping around . . ."

"I'm a police officer," said Lance.

"You're a joke."

"I'm a police officer, and that actually does give me certain rights. And obligations."

"A *police officer?* You're the guy who picks up the empty bottles left behind after other people's parties. That's basically what you've always done."

"Well, at least I've always picked up after *you.*"

"Yeah, right."

"Like with Clayton Miller."

Andy sat up with a jolt, as if he couldn't believe what he'd just heard.

"*Clayton Miller?* What does he have to do with anything?"

"The kid you almost killed? I was the one who stopped you. If it weren't for me, you would have—"

"That old story?" said Andy. "We were just fighting. That's all."

"I *saw* you—"

"So what?"

"It's no good trying to talk your way out of it. I was there. I saw what you've got inside of you. So don't come here and talk to me about empty bottles, because I'm the one who's always cleaning up your *shit*."

They were glaring at each other now. For a moment Lance thought Andy was going to punch him. He could feel the adrenaline race through his body. His hands were shaking.

"You don't know shit," said Andy.

"You already said that."

"But let me tell you one thing," his brother went on. "If you really want to play at being a cop, don't do it with your own family."

"What do you mean by that?"

"You broke into my cabin. And that's all I'm going to say."

"Not that bullshit again."

"Don't you think I realized it was you from the very beginning?"

Lance made a point of not shifting his gaze, but his face felt unnaturally tense.

"It was one thing when you said you tried to find the key first. But when I got inside . . . I could tell it was you from a mile away. Just from how the place was *halfheartedly* vandalized."

"I'm not the only one who knows where you used to keep the key," said Lance. "What about Chrissy? She's seventeen now. Isn't it more likely that some kids, including your daughter, broke the cabin window because they didn't find the key where it was supposed to be? And then later on the party got out of hand?"

"Sure, and that's why there were no broken beer bottles or puke," said Andy. "But you didn't think of that, did you?

You should have thrown up in a few places before you left. Or peed on the floor. But you've got no talent for that kind of thing. You have no idea how to get shitfaced."

"But I *know* she was there," said Lance. He no longer cared how this was going to end.

"Bullshit! We both know you were the one who did it."

"Okay, you're right. I was the one who broke in, but that's not what I'm talking about now."

Andy smiled warily.

"I know Chrissy was there with you . . . on the night of the murder."

Andy's expression changed without warning. His face suddenly turned ashen. He looked like he wanted to say something. He opened his mouth several times, but not a sound came out.

"So you're the one who needs to watch out," Lance went on. He pressed his palms against his thighs, trying to hide the fact that his hands were shaking.

Andy grabbed his backpack and opened the Jeep door. He got out, not hurrying, as if everything were perfectly normal. But he didn't say a word. Then he proceeded to slip his arms through the straps of his backpack. Lance tried to see his eyes under the Minnesota Twins cap, but he couldn't. After Andy put on his backpack he closed the door. Not too hard and not too soft, just the same way he always did. Then he walked over to his own vehicle. Lance got out too. He looked at his brother over the roof of the Jeep. Andy took out his Winchester and slung it over his shoulder. Then he closed the red-painted right-hand door of his old white Chevy and started walking across the parking lot.

"Are we going to keep hunting?" asked Lance, but he wasn't sure Andy heard him. "Are we going to keep hunting?" he repeated, this time so loudly his brother couldn't avoid hearing. But Andy didn't reply. He headed across the parking area and disappeared into the woods.

Lance exhaled slowly. He wasn't even aware he'd been holding his breath. In front of him was Lake Superior, which almost merged with the gray sky. On his left was the dense birch forest Andy had just entered. On his right he could see the start of the path that led to Baraga's Cross. Early one morning in the summer, he'd found a shoe lying there. A white running shoe. Lance had picked it up. That was how it had all started.

He wondered what he should do now. Andy had headed for the open area along the lakeshore, the spot where he'd said he would wait on post. It was only a couple of hundred yards away, close to the crime scene. Should he try to call Andy on his cell? No, he hadn't replied when they were talking in person, so why would he answer his phone? Lance decided that, no matter what, it would be best to complete the drive; then at least he would have done his part.

After he got back in the Jeep and was about to drive off, he hesitated for a moment. Couldn't he just go home? Send Andy a text to say he didn't feel like hunting anymore? But that would be a form of retreat, and he couldn't do that, not after he'd just pushed Andy into a corner. Because that was what he'd done. His brother hadn't been able to utter a single word. He'd just sat there, gaping, his face gray. Lance couldn't retreat now.

Slowly he drove up the narrow Baraga Cross Road and onto Highway 61. It was no more than two miles to the Temperance River. He'd park the Jeep there and then walk through the woods between the road and the lake, back to the parking lot near Baraga's Cross. He wasn't counting on riding back with Andy to get his car afterward, but he could easily manage those two miles along Highway 61 on foot. He'd finish the hunt as planned, but then that would be it.

I dreamed about Jesus waking up the dead. They came walking in a big procession down toward the dock on Toftevågen. Jesus led the way. Behind him came the teacher and the pastor, and behind those two everybody else. A bunch of partially rotted scarecrows. They seemed to be mostly women, since so many had long hair. But Jesus did too. Long, golden hair and a red beard. He was carrying an oar on each shoulder. He was going to row everybody across the ocean to America. And in the middle of the group heading for the dock I caught sight of the Indian. There he was, walking along with those who had been resurrected. I wanted to tell Jesus that there was a heathen in their midst, but he gave me a clout with one of the oars, making my ears ring. You, said Jesus, looking furious as he pointed at me, you are not coming with us to the New World. The heathen will take your place in the boat. But why? I asked. I have always prayed to you and kept your name sacred. Yes, you have, said Jesus, but the savage is so good at rowing. If it weren't for that, you probably could have come along.

All I could do was stand there and watch as the teacher and the pastor and the Indian went over to the edge of the dock and then disappeared. Because there was no boat. The whole pack of skeletons dropped over the side of the dock. Jesus did too, carrying those long oars over his shoulders. After everyone had stepped off the edge of the dock and vanished, I went over there and looked down. In my dream it looked completely different. The water was very deep. And then I saw them. Way down in the water they were rowing a handsome ship toward the open sea. Jesus stood in the bow, with his golden hair blowing back like a banner. He had handed over the oars. Now it was the dead who had to row. The Indian was sitting there too. He was going to America, even though I was being left behind at home. That thought frightened me awake.

I'm still inside his sod hut. He's squatting down next to the fire and stirring his brew. When he bends down over the pot, I can see his face, black from smoke and soot, or whatever else might have left streaks like that. His eyes under the brim of his hat look like otter eyes. Now he is sitting down in the corner again. Wrapping the blanket around him. The smell must be coming from what he's cooking. It smells like . . . I'm not exactly sure what. Like hay? Yes, a bit like hay, but there's something else too, something I can't identify. Something sweet and strange. Maybe it's the steam rising up from his brew that is making me dream like this. Is that where the dreams are coming from? This is not a Christian home, at least. How strange that I should end up here. Thormod Olson from Tofte on Halsnøy. Dear Jesus, am I going to die in this un-Christian lair? No! It's not far to where my uncle lives. I don't remember him, because it was so long ago that he set off for America, but we are family. He is my mother's brother. I can't die now, not when I'm so close to where I'm headed.

But the cold floods through me again. It's coming from a lump of ice. I must have swallowed it when I fell in, and it's still inside me. Refusing to melt. Lying there, spreading its cold. Now my teeth start to chatter. I'm shaking all over. The Indian is stirring under the blanket over in the corner. He crawls over to me. Gets up on his knees. Under the fur rug I'm still gripping the ax handle in my right hand. With my left I'm holding the rug in place. I don't want him to see me naked again, or start rubbing me. He's saying something.

I think it's English, but it's not the sort of English I'm used to hearing. He's not as old as I thought. Younger than my father, I think. He puts his hand on my forehead. That warm hand of his. Then he raises his index finger and shakes it, repeating the same word over and over. A warning? I think he's saying that I should not get up. That I should stay where I am. He stands up and moves the birchbark door aside. Shakes his finger at me one last time. Then he slips out and pulls the sheet of bark in place. I hear the first steps he takes on the packed snow. Then it's quiet.

What's he up to? Going to take a shit, maybe? Or are there others like him nearby? Is he going out to get the neighbors? And here I lie, naked as a newborn babe and shaking so hard I can't even put on my clothes, much less defend myself. I keep thinking I'm going to die here. I won't survive this, not as cold as I am. I'm going to die in the savage's sod hut. And then I won't be given a Christian burial. Does that mean I'll go to hell? A boy like me, who believes in God and Jesus Christ. A boy like me, who believes in the Resurrection. But God must know this. He knows everything, after all. But is it necessary to be buried in consecrated ground in order to go to heaven? I don't know. All I know is that I need to get out of here as soon as possible. Make my way to where my uncle Knut and Nanette live. If I die there, I will be buried as a Christian. This is all about my soul. That's what is happening here inside this hut. A battle for my eternal soul. "A human being consists of an eternal soul and a mortal body," said the pastor. Yet if my body dies and my soul lives on, but without reaching paradise, what will happen then? Even if I have to crawl on my belly out of this hut and through the woods, like a snake wriggling along the ground, I refuse to die here. I refuse! How long is he going to be gone? Do I have time to find my clothes? I can't crawl naked over the snow, but I don't know if I have the strength to get dressed.

I let go of the ax and try to roll closer to the fire. I feel a gnawing inside me. That must be the broken rib. The stumps are gnawing at each other. I lose my hold on the fur rug, and it drops off me. I am naked in the light from the fire. "In the beginning there was no sin in the world, for all that God had created was good, but our first parents allowed the Devil to tempt them into sinning." I feel a warmth on the surface of my skin. It's coming from the flames that are right in front of me. It felt so good when he rubbed me with that dried grass. I look down at myself. I feel an urge to find the grass and rub myself with it. But what if he comes back inside and sees me? No, I couldn't live with that. Anything would be better than that. I crawl a little closer to the fire, but I can't stop shaking. The pot is hanging from a stick. The witch's brew is bubbling away. The smell reminds me of long hay racks on an embankment. Drying hay. With something sweet inside, but I can't tell what it is. My face is wet and blazing hot. Steam is running in big drops down my cheek. What could he have put in that pot? I saw him crumbling something into it. I don't know. The whole world seems to have turned upside down and is spinning around inside my head. I close my eyes. When I open them again, I see my clothes. They're lying over there in the darkest corner. I crawl over to them. The homespun cloth is ice-cold and rigid, like old leather. I don't know whether I can even get the clothes on, they're so stiff. Why didn't he put my clothes next to the fire? So I wouldn't run away?

I try to put on my shirt. It still bears the cold from the lake, but I force myself to put it on. It feels like being covered with ice. But it's impossible to put on my underwear. I can't bend down far enough. I see how awful it is that I'm naked. With everything in full view. Now that I've put on my shirt, I see that so clearly. My hand touches something soft. It's the bunch of dried grass that he used to rub warmth into my body. I throw the grass into the flames. It catches fire instantly and burns up. So that sin is now gone. No matter whether I sit or stand, it's impossible for me to pull my pants over my feet because of my broken rib. I can't do it. Here I am, on my knees, naked from the waist down. I can't allow anyone to see me like this. But what's that over in the corner, next to the blanket the savage left? It's dark, so I creep over there on all fours, like an animal. I reach out one hand to touch the blanket. It's still warm from his body. But what's that lying on the ground next to my other hand? I touch it. Yes, just what I thought. A rifle. Cautiously I pick it up. Weigh it in my hands.

LANCE TURNED OFF THE ENGINE, pulled up his hood, and got out. By now he'd waited fifteen minutes, as they'd agreed. He left his backpack on the passenger seat, since there was no more food inside anyway, but he did take out the small flashlight he always kept in the Jeep and stuck it in his jacket pocket. Then he opened the tailgate and took out his rifle, which was wrapped in the brown blanket. The wrench lay in the same place it had landed when Andy tossed it back inside. There was something so unreal about the bloody tuft of white fur, as if it couldn't possibly belong in his life. He slammed the tailgate shut and then crossed the asphalt parking lot, taking long, determined strides.

When he reached the edge of the woods, he stopped and took several deep breaths. Then he entered the forest.

Right below him was the lake. The rocks were slippery and treacherous in rainy weather; he needed to avoid them. If he fell in the water, who knew how it would end? Behind him was the Temperance River. It was black and deep as it flowed between two rock walls, as if through a doorway, and out to the lake.

There were often deer down here, so maybe they'd get one after all. But what are we going to do afterward? Lance wondered. If he shot a deer now, could he really call Andy on his cell and ask him to join him? Could he phone Andy for any reason at all? He would have to do that in order to complete the drive. The driver always had to contact the man on post to let him know he was approaching. That was an inviolable rule. But were the rules still valid after what had happened? Was it even possible to talk about things like rules anymore? Lance had broken the most important rule of all, which said that specific subjects were simply not to be discussed. Not under any circumstances. The world he knew was a world that was held together by keeping silent about certain things. These things were not clearly defined, but everybody who lived in the same world as Lance recognized them at once whenever they cropped up. As long as no one broke the rule, this world would continue to exist. It had already endured for a very long time. But now Lance had talked. He had opened his mouth and declared that the most important rule of all was no longer valid. And so he couldn't expect that other rules were still valid either.

He paused near a birch tree and leaned against the trunk, causing a shower of drops to fall from the branches and pour down over him, but he hardly noticed. Should he turn around and go back to the parking lot? Drive home?

There was no rule, after all, that said he had to complete the drive. He *could* call it quits and head home. But he didn't because it wouldn't change anything. No matter what, Andy knew that he knew. It made no difference whether Lance was here or at home in his own living room. He'll find me if he wants to, he thought. The only chance Lance had was to disappear entirely from the world they both knew. Outside that world, there was no certainty Andy would be able to find him.

His cell phone vibrated against his thigh. Lance's hand shook as he took it out. Mary's number was on the display. She seldom called, and if she did, it was always about some practical matter having to do with picking up or dropping off their son, Jimmy. But Lance wasn't supposed to have the boy until next weekend, so it was more likely that Jimmy was the one calling him now.

Lance and Andy had agreed not to take calls from anyone else. Not under any circumstance. But the rules probably didn't count anymore. For all Lance knew, his brother wasn't even on post. So of course he would take his son's call. He was just about to answer when he hesitated. He wasn't really sure why. It had nothing to do with the hunt or the rules. There was just something that stopped him from answering. In his mind he pictured his seven-year-old son. Each time the phone vibrated in his hand, he thought about the sound in the boy's ear. Finally it stopped. He put the phone back in his pocket. He felt bad, but not as bad as he'd expected.

I'm out here hunting, he told himself. That was his way of trying to preserve some small trace of normality. Hunting was something he'd mastered. At this moment it was the only thing he felt he'd mastered. He was a good marksman. And right now that was something he still counted on. He started walking again. Soon he found fresh deer scat.

It wasn't possible to see any tracks since the forest floor was too hard for that, but he thought he could see a clearing in the woods a short way up ahead. In such places it was common to encounter deer. That was where they grazed. And if they weren't grazing, they would still be hidden by the tall grass.

Cautiously Lance approached the clearing, ready to raise his rifle and shoot at a moment's notice. Before taking each step, he studied the forest floor carefully so as not to tread on a dry twig or get his boot caught on something that would cause him to fall. Then he would again raise his head, lift his foot from the ground, and slowly move it forward while he kept an eye on the gaps between the trees. At any time a deer might leap up from where it was lying in the grass and stand there with all its senses on high alert. When that happened he had to raise the rifle to his shoulder, find the animal in the scope, and fire off a lethal shot—all in the space of a few seconds, without vacillating or hesitating. The way he was proceeding made for a minimum of sound. His movements were also so slow as to be almost invisible. After each step he would stand motionless for up to a minute at a time, and for that reason it took him several minutes to cover only a few yards. It was approximately fifty yards to the clearing, which he could partially make out between the tree trunks. If he were to continue forward at this pace, it would take him over half an hour, but he wasn't going to do that. In front of him was an invisible borderline. If nothing happened before he reached that spot, it was unlikely any deer would appear.

He crossed the invisible border and started walking at a more normal pace, but still moving cautiously and holding his rifle so he'd be ready to shoot. Over by the clearing, which was bigger than he'd at first thought, he immediately found the hollowed-out places where three deer had been lying in the grass. He crouched down to study them. They seemed fresh; a few rough hairs had been left behind. It was impossible to tell in which direction the deer had gone. It would probably be best for Lance to go down to the lake where the forest was not as dense so he could get a better overview.

He started walking and soon reached the bare rocks, but there was nothing to see. The rain had stopped. He pushed back his hood. The sky was still low and gray. From here it was normally possible to see smoke pouring from the chimneys of the coal-fired power plant in Taconite Harbor, a few miles farther along the shore. But today Lance saw only the expanse of black, wet rocks right in front of him and the gray surface of the water. He sat down at the edge of the rocks. Far off in the distance there was a spot where the water was 1,332 feet deep. That was in the southeastern part of the lake, as he seemed to recall, off the coast of Michigan. Far from here, at any rate.

He wondered whether anyone had ever actually gone down there. In a diving bell, for instance. Or had that happened only once, in a dream? And who was it that had stood down there back then? A white American or an Ojibwe? Who was he really when he stood there, about to freeze into a pillar of ice? That dream was so different from any he'd ever had before. Presumably it was those kinds of dreams that the Ojibwe turned into important elements in their lives. Big, far-reaching dreams that clearly had some meaning for a person. Was that why he no longer dreamed at all? Because he'd allowed the big dream in his life to go unused?

I have to tell Willy about this, he thought. That seemed so obvious, and yet the thought had never occurred to him until now. Of course Willy was the only one who could help him bring the dream to life again. It was dead because he'd never bothered to make use of it, had never acknowledged it, and so it had solidified, freezing into something as hard as a rock and blocking the path for all other dreams. That's what he would tell Willy. He would just have to risk having the old man laugh at him, but something told him that wouldn't happen.

"*I dreamed that I found a wooden figure of two people holding hands,*" Willy had said. What was that supposed to mean? Maybe he'd just made it all up so he could tell the story about Swamper Caribou's knife. But if that was true, it was a poor excuse. Willy couldn't even remember what it was about the dream that had made him think of the old story. No doubt the dream and the story had nothing to do with each other—yet upon further thought, they might. Both were about finding something. And about two people who were linked to each other. The two holding hands, in the shape of a tree root; and the two brothers who had been so alike that it was hard to tell them apart. Joe and Swamper Caribou.

Lance had an old photograph of Joe in the archives that belonged to the local historical society. But as far as he knew, there was no picture of Swamper. Regardless, how was he, Lance Hansen, supposed to know what a dream like that meant? Or whether it meant anything at all? He felt stupid for even having such a thought. He was a police officer, and interpreting dreams was not part of his job description. I don't even believe dreams are important, he thought, but he knew that was a lie. The truth was that he knew better than most people how important dreams were. He missed waking up from a dream. He missed it more than being physically touched.

Hardly anybody touched Lance anymore; only his son. He wondered what the boy wanted when he phoned. Because it had to have been Jimmy, and not Mary. The boy had tried to call his father, but Lance hadn't answered. And he knew why: *because he was in the process of disappearing.* He might as well get his son used to the idea sooner rather than later. Maybe he wouldn't come back at all. He hoped he would, but there was no guarantee. He didn't even know where he was going, just that he was in the process of disappearing from the world he knew. Jimmy's world. Mary's. His mother's.

Lance raised his rifle and used the scope to survey the shoreline, but he saw only the gray lake, gray sky, naked trees, and the expanse of rock, dark with rain. If he tried to look out at the open waters, the clouds and lake merged, making it impossible to tell which was which. But as long as he let his gaze slide along the land, he was able to see quite far. Through the light drizzle he caught a glimpse of the ten-foot-tall cross at the very tip, near the mouth of the Cross River. But he couldn't see much farther than that.

The cross had stood there since 1846, when Father Frederic Baraga came ashore there after a boat trip that had nearly cost him his life. Grateful to be alive, he had raised a cross consisting of two birch branches that he had lashed together. Eight years later a new wooden cross was erected, replaced in the 1930s by the present granite cross.

Lance's father had taught him to remain vigilant when nothing was happening, to listen when there was silence. He now did what he had learned. He got up and slowly began walking. Stopped often. Stood still and listened, but he heard nothing except the rain striking his clothing and the sound of an occasional car passing by up on the road. He knew he mustn't lose focus, not for a second. If I do, he thought, I don't stand a chance.

It began with a light touch, which he barely noticed. He grabbed hold of a birch branch to bend it aside and felt ice under his fingertips. A thin layer that melted from the touch of his hand. He took a closer look at the branch. Frost covered the extremity. When he checked the other branches nearby, he saw the same thing. The sections where rain had struck were now covered with ice. It was thin and difficult to see, but once he noticed it, he saw ice everywhere. The trees all around him had acquired a sheen that they hadn't had only a few minutes ago.

More raindrops kept pelting the already ice-covered branches. They froze instantly. The ice grew thicker as he stood there. He was all too familiar with the phenomenon of freezing rain and how it happened: precipitation that falls through a subfreezing layer of air and is supercooled to below freezing, yet continues in liquid form as long at it doesn't hit anything solid. It's the same thing that makes the water in a lake start freezing along the edges instead of in the middle. Freezing rain was a common weather phenomenon along Lake Superior. In its most extreme version, it's called an ice storm.

Lance had experienced several ice storms, but it had been a few years since the last one. He especially recalled the time in the mid-1970s when all of Duluth stood still for a couple of days. The power went out, and they had to cook their food in the fireplace. Schools were closed. And there was a strict ban on going outdoors because of all the power lines that had been downed by the weight of the ice. Some of them sent sparks into the nighttime darkness. He could see it from his room, since from there he had a good view of a large part of the city. It seemed even more dangerous because the lights and the furnace were no longer working in his house. Or in any of the other houses, either. Yet sparks flew out from the ice-laden wires that sagged to the ground. The power hadn't actually gone; it was just no longer under control. It had changed from being a basic necessity, which people simply took for granted, to a lethal and unpredictable force.

Lance ran his hand over the barrel of his rifle several times in order to prevent it from icing over. His own body was too warm to allow ice to form on him, but he noticed that something that looked like slush had started to settle in the creases of his jacket sleeves. That was nothing to worry about; he just needed to keep going. He started walking again. He hadn't yet heard the sound of ice striking ice, but he had a feeling he soon would. He had no problem moving forward since the forest floor wasn't slippery. But it was probably already extremely dangerous to be traversing the rocks along the shore of the lake. He slung the strap of his rifle over his shoulder and rubbed his hands as he walked, trying to warm them up, but it didn't help much.

The sound of the rain had changed. He didn't know why, but he could hear the difference quite clearly. Was that the sound of water freezing to ice as it struck the branches and rocks around him? It had a higher pitch than ordinary rain. The grass and leaves underfoot were starting to crackle with a more brittle sound than before. Aside from that crackling and the pelting of the rain, there were no other sounds as he walked. Andy was right when he'd said they'd have the forest to themselves down here. Maybe Andy wasn't even here anymore. It was possible Lance was the only one in this part of the woods at the moment.

Even though he couldn't see it, he was aware that the ice was getting thicker with every raindrop that fell. After a while he took the rifle from his shoulder to inspect it. A thin layer of ice had formed along the underside of the barrel, which was the part that had been turned upward as he walked with the gun over his shoulder. He ran his hand back and forth over the barrel until all of the ice had melted away. There was also ice underneath the trigger guard. He used his thumb to clear it off. As long as he kept to the dense forest, not much rain would strike his rifle. Most of it was settling high up in the birch trees. The thick interlacing of branches overhead was getting more and more shiny. If he happened to run into a tree trunk, a shower of water no longer dripped from the branches. The water had turned to ice.

He again slung the strap of his rifle over his shoulder and continued on. The sounds had changed once more; now he noticed that a faint clinking undertone, barely audible, had crept in. It must be coming from the impact of the rain on the most slender twigs, causing them to move slightly. Ice striking ice. He remembered how back in the seventies the weather had finally broken after an ice storm lasting a couple of days. The temperature rose and a wind started to blow. The ice hanging from the trees clinked and clanked in the gusts like some strange, avant-garde music. Yet that time it had a whole different dimension. Yard-long icicles swung in the wind. Lots of trees had broken in half in the city parks. The shattered trunks were visible from far off, standing there with their fresh, light-colored wood exposed.

Now Lance noticed that he could no longer hear any cars passing by on Highway 61. In fact, he hadn't heard any for quite a while. The few people who were out driving on this gray, rainy Sunday afternoon must have pulled over to take a break somewhere along the highway. The surface of the road must already be slippery as hell, and he probably wouldn't be able to drive back home afterward. Not that it mattered, because he still didn't have a sense that there was going to be any "afterward." The only thing that felt real was continuing to walk through the woods as the ice grew thicker all around him. It was becoming more visible too. Little lumps of ice were forming on the branches.

The next time he took off his rifle to look at it, he saw that a new layer of ice had settled on the underside of the barrel and the trigger guard. Now it was noticeably thicker, and he had to spend more time rubbing it off. His hands got so cold he had to pause and stuff them in his pockets. He took a short break but then had to go back to running his hand along the barrel. Finally he'd managed to de-ice the gun and could sling it back on his shoulder.

The rain was still coming down steadily, and every single one of the endless drops froze the instant it hit the ground or the trees. He could actually see the ice growing right before his eyes. The tree branches were encapsulated in icy holsters that were getting thicker and thicker. Now it seemed like there was no one else in the whole world in this forest. No outside sounds were audible. The only thing he heard was a muted clinking, as if an infinite number of tiny glass beads were just barely glancing off one another.

Then his phone started vibrating again. Lance took it out and looked at the number on the display. It was Andy. The idea of hearing his voice seemed so unreal. As if he were receiving a call from the other side. He had to pull himself together before he could answer.

"Hello?"

Silence on the other end.

"Hello?" he repeated.

He thought he could hear something, maybe the wind.

"Andy?"

No, it had to be the sound of his brother's stifled breathing.

"Can we talk, Andy?"

Then the connection was cut.

Lance stood there a moment longer with the phone pressed to his ear, as if waiting for something to happen. Then he called Andy back. He counted the ring tones. After the phone had rung ten times, he gave up and put the cell back in his pocket.

The sound of ice touching ice had grown louder. Maybe only because the rain was coming down harder. On the phone he hadn't heard any sounds other than his brother breathing, if that was actually what he'd heard. In any case, no voices or any traffic noise in the background. There was no traffic now anyway, and Andy would never think of driving in these conditions. If he tried, he wouldn't even be able to make it out of the parking lot and up to the main road. He's still here in the woods, thought Lance. Though it was impossible to say where. Maybe he was on post, as they'd agreed, but he could just as well be very close by. The only thing Lance was sure of was that his brother was out there somewhere.

No matter what, he couldn't just stay in one spot, so he started walking, with a noticeable reluctance in his body, as if he had to persuade part of himself to keep going. Every time he touched a branch, it rattled with ice. Small icicles had started to form. The biggest were no longer than his little finger, but they kept on growing. It was impossible not to make a sound as he moved because the forest was so dense, but if he chose to walk along the lake, where the terrain was more open, he'd be more visible, and that would be worse. He remembered the feeling he'd had that someone was aiming at him as he stood at the top of the big boulder, completely exposed. He didn't want to subject himself to anything like that again, so he continued making his way through the birch forest.

He was no longer deer hunting; this was something different. Moving among the trees that were becoming increasingly covered with ice, heading toward his brother, who was somewhere up ahead. Occasionally he caught sight of the lake through openings in the woods. He thought about the expanse of rocks, where the glittering ice must have settled in an even layer that was barely visible. Anyone who set so much as one foot on that treacherous surface would immediately fall into the water. The difference between the vegetation and the slippery ground could quickly become the difference between life and death. Because how could anyone manage to climb back out? There was practically nothing but rocks along the lake between the Temperance and the Cross Rivers.

Yet there was something enticing about the sporadic glimpses of the huge gray surface of water. Lance had an urge to see those treacherous rocks. Finally he gave in and headed back down. Only when he emerged from the woods did he realize how hard it was actually raining. The drops pelted his hood. He involuntarily ducked, as if that might help. In front of him was a six-foot-wide belt of grass and heath, before the naked expanse of rocks began. With a couple more steps the tips of his boots touched the ice. The fact that it was almost invisible made it even more treacherous. If someone didn't know the ground was covered with ice, it would be easy to miss, since it was so transparent. A strange-looking sheen was the only sign that everything was not normal.

Lance lifted his right foot, letting it hover an inch or two above the ground. Then he slowly lowered it until his boot was just barely touching the ice, while keeping all of his weight on the other foot. He stood there like that for a few seconds before he cautiously shifted a little weight onto the foot on the ice. It instantly slid forward. Since he was prepared for this, he remained in full control, but it made him nervous to think what might have happened if he had unsuspectingly stepped out onto the rocks.

He went back to the woods and continued in the same direction as before, heading for the Cross River and Baraga's Cross. The ice got thicker, the icicles longer, clattering louder as he walked. In one spot he found a row of extra big icicles hanging at eye level. They were as long as his index finger, but thinner. In the closest icicle he could see a hazy reflection of his surroundings. When he leaned forward, he saw his face. It was so distorted as to be unrecognizable, but there was no doubt he was looking at his own reflection in the ice. He pulled his head back for a moment and then leaned close again. The movement made his face change shape, alternately compressed and expanded. It looked like it was shouting from inside, but without a voice.

As he turned away to keep going, his shoulder brushed against a branch. For a moment it sounded like a set of little chimes. In his mind he pictured the skeleton at the bottom of Lake Superior. The sound of ice bones. When Lance looked up again, he caught sight of him. The man was standing between the ice-covered birch trees, barely twenty yards away, with his head bent forward slightly so that his big, round hat covered most of his face. Lance had known this would happen sooner or later. The man had on the same miserable old clothes that he'd worn when Lance saw him a few months ago. His jacket and pants were both shiny with age and looked like they were several sizes too big. His jacket had probably been a suit jacket once upon a time. The brim of his hat drooped, as if the hat had been in the water for a long time and was now about to dissolve. The man looked like a figure that had accidentally stepped out of an old black-and-white photograph. No, not accidentally. It was more like he possessed a force of will that could overwhelm any resistance, even the impenetrable barrier of time itself.

Lance didn't want to move. He just stood there, looking at the man, who also remained motionless. How long they stood like that, he couldn't tell. He was no longer aware of the passage of time. At last the man slowly raised his head so that his face gradually came into view under the brim of his hat. The face of a full-blooded Ojibwe. It was soot-covered, as if he'd spent a long time bending forward as he sat next to a fire. Lance felt his gaze like a weight on his chest that got heavier and colder. Swamper Caribou looked as if he hadn't slept properly for a very long time. His face was swollen and drawn. Lance could hear the sound of ice getting thicker and thicker all around them, while he himself got heavier and colder. It occurred to him that he was dying. That was the reason for this sense of heaviness and cold.

The Indian started coming toward him. Lance tried desperately to lift his feet in an attempt to turn around, but it was no use. His body no longer obeyed him. Swamper Caribou kept coming closer. Nothing in his face changed. It was without expression. Finally he was standing only a couple of yards away. Water dripped from his hat brim and ran from the sleeves of his jacket. The strands of hair that stuck out from under his hat looked soaked. He raised his right arm and held it out to Lance. His hand was open, his fingers spread. Now his face changed too. He looked desperate, as if he were pleading for something.

Lance felt the weight leave his body. He could move again. When he realized this, all of the suppressed fear raced to every crevice of his body, and he spun on his heel and ran as fast as he could. He heard the unrelenting sound of raindrops, ice, and branches striking his hood. Then, all of a sudden, he heard only rain. He'd emerged from the forest. Ahead of him lay the lake and the treacherous rocks. He turned around and pulled his rifle off his shoulder. A cold shock passed from his hands to the rest of his body. The gun was completely coated with ice. He tried to chamber a round, but the mechanism wouldn't budge. The same thing happened with the safety; he couldn't release it. The rifle was unusable.

Nothing moved at the edge of the woods. The Indian hadn't followed him. And Lance hadn't really thought he would. He turned back toward the lake and took a couple of steps forward. In front of his boots was the borderline between solid ground and death. There was no doubt in his mind that he would die if he took another step. He would slide right down into the lake. Even if the fall didn't knock him unconscious, he would never be able to climb back out of the water. Then Lake Superior would finally engulf him, for the first and last time. And that actually seemed right. In what other depths did he belong but here?

In a sense it felt like *this* was the bottom of the lake. He looked around. This ice world. But if that was true, where would he end up now if he fell into the water and sank? Would he emerge from the lake into a radiant, hot summer day on the other side? Boats plowing stripes of white wake water, American flags fluttering in the breeze, cars driving along Highway 61? The normal world in which he could get into his Jeep and drive down to Two Harbors to visit his brother. And afterward go home to Mary and Jimmy. Sit on the sofa with them and watch TV. Lie in bed next to Mary. Sleep. Dream. Wake up like a normal man.

The cold from the rifle was stinging his hands. He slung it over his shoulder again. The rain was still pouring down, and every drop froze to ice the moment it struck something solid. There was no sign of life, only a shadowy figure who didn't belong in the same world with him.

Lance stuck his cold hands in his jacket pockets. His right hand touched something. He took it out. It was a Dove chocolate. For a moment he felt a great resistance to unwrapping the paper to see what the message was inside. He felt an urge to hurl the little heart into the trees. Yet his curiosity was equally strong, and finally it won out.

6

I don't even know how long he's been gone. Or whether time is passing quickly or slowly. I'm sitting on the floor holding his rifle on my lap. Wearing only my shirt, which has started to thaw out a bit, but it still feels like I have a shell of ice around me. Below I'm completely naked. I need to put on the rest of my clothes and get away before he comes back, but my rib hurts so bad when I bend down that I can't pull on my pants. If I don't get out of here, I'm going to end up in hell. And there I will burn for all eternity. With no boat or house, only sinners and flames. But I'll be all right if I can only reach Knut and Nanette. If I do that, I will spend the rest of my days living as a true Christian should. "I believe in the Holy Spirit, the holy Christian church, the communion of saints, the forgiveness of sins, the resurrection of the body, and the life everlasting. All men will no doubt be resurrected and live on after death, but only those who, through the grace of the Holy Spirit, keep their faith in Jesus Christ, can hope for joyous resurrection and blessed everlasting life." All else is eternal torment.

I'm holding the rifle so tight that I've almost lost all feeling in my hands. Or is the cold to blame? If I'm going to put on the rest of my clothes, I need to set down the gun. I don't know whether I dare risk doing that. Because then I'll be defenseless. No, I can't set it down. What if he comes back and I have no gun? Then I'll never get out of here. He won't let me go. That was why he put my clothes in the darkest corner, far away from the fire, so I wouldn't be able to get dressed again. I don't know why he's keeping me here, but I can't die in this hut. Then I'll go straight to hell. So I can't put down the rifle. I just have to sit here, holding it on my lap, until he comes back. But what am I going to do then? Maybe I can manage to put my pants on first. He might be gone for a while yet. But then I'll have to set down the gun. And then I'll be defenseless. I came to America to get a boat and a house. I can't die here. And now . . . there . . . now I heard . . . wasn't that the sound of someone coughing?

As I lay in the dark and listened to the clear singing of angels in Paradise, I saw the whole hut turn golden in a flash of light, and the rifle was hovering in midair, as if it were alive. I saw it over and over, many times. Again and again. I saw no Indian, just the golden hut and the rifle floating in the air. And the whole time the angels were singing. It was a song I'd never heard before. I almost believed I'd gone to Heaven. Did I die? I wondered about this as I lay over there in the corner. My head felt empty, as if someone had blown everything out through my ears. Am I dead now? I wondered. Are those angels singing in Paradise? But gradually the song changed into this pinging sound that never stops. There is a pinging in my ears. A pinging from one ear to the other, as if a string is stretched between them. A string that is trembling and pinging inside my head.

I open my eyes and see that I'm still here in the Indian's hut. I notice a bad, sharp smell. The rifle is lying on the floor. Sticking out from under the big piece of birch bark covering the doorway I see an arm and a hand. When I blink my eyes I still see the gun hovering in the air, but now it is a bluish shadow in a white room. Why is it floating in the air, as if it were alive? I get onto all fours and crawl over to the gun. Hold it in my hands. The barrel is warm. I look toward the doorway. There is no longer an arm sticking out from under the bark. I must have shot the Indian, but he's not dead. Oh Jesus, save me! Now he's waiting for me outside the hut. I've seen that he wears a knife on his belt. If I poke my head out, I'll be slaughtered like a lamb. Did I do it on purpose? No, I just squeezed the trigger. I heard something and so I squeezed the trigger. But I had to do it, because he wasn't going to let me go. And now he means to get me. Not a sound from outside, but soon he'll come back with his knife. It's now or never, Thormod.

LANCE WASN'T POSITIVE that it was here Georg Lofthus had been killed—the whole dense birch forest looked much the same—but it *felt* like this was the place. Here he'd caught sight of the naked body between the trunks of the birches. This is where it all started, he thought. That was why he felt this sudden chill, as if he'd fallen into a deep hole. A raw, iron cold. His rifle was slung over his shoulder, transformed into an ice sculpture. Inside the sculpture he could still glimpse the dark shape of the gun.

He closed his eyes and let the world contract to the clinking sound of the rain falling onto the ice-coated forest. As he stood there like that, a great calm descended over him, as if this was where he belonged. He remembered how he'd stood in the parking lot afterward with the local police officers, feeling that the horror back there inside the woods belonged to him and no one else. Every time someone went in there, they seemed to take something away from him. At first the sight of that shattered head had been his alone, but soon everyone had taken a look at it, snapping photographs and jotting down comments in black notebooks. Now this place was his again, just as it had been in the beginning.

When Lance opened his eyes, everything looked just the same as before he'd closed them, but he knew that in the meantime the ice had gotten thicker. With every added layer it grew, he became more and more cut off from the rest of the world. For every drop of rain that fell, the forest became a bit more insulated from outside sounds. Little by little it got harder to push the branches aside, and the path back home got longer. He almost couldn't believe his house even existed anymore. Or his possessions. The family photographs. The drawings Jimmy had given him. He thought about the phone call; the boy must have been trying to get ahold of him. But he didn't regret the fact that he hadn't answered. Where he was going, he couldn't be reached.

Lance raised his hand and cautiously touched a few of the icicles, making them move with a delicate ringing sound. He did it again, harder this time, and touching more icicles, as if he were playing many tiny, untuned chimes. He kept on doing that, at the same slow tempo of a funeral march. Then he began to worry and stopped. Somebody might hear.

Suddenly he pictured his father's face. Oscar was sitting at the kitchen table at home in Duluth. Behind him was the window facing Fifth Avenue. It was spring, and the snow was melting on the sidewalks. Sunlight had formed a halo around his father's head. "He's lying to us, you know," Oscar Hansen said. "He's . . . *a liar.*"

"You have no right to talk that way about your own son," replied his mother quietly. As usual, she was somewhere else in the room, not sitting at the table. Only Lance and his father were sitting there. Lance couldn't see himself; he saw only what he would have seen on that spring day long ago: his father's face and Fifth Avenue outside the window behind him. The melting snow on the sidewalks.

Suddenly his father slammed his fist down on the table, making all the plates and silverware jump. "I refuse to let him hang out with those kids!" he shouted at the top of his lungs.

As he stood there in the icy forest many years later, Lance could still feel the impact of that long-ago shout. Yet this was something he'd completely forgotten. He must have been about eighteen when it happened. Andy was sixteen. His father had called Andy a liar. He didn't remember what that was about. Someone he wasn't supposed to associate with. Andy used to hang out in Lester Park with his pals. They would take along a boom box and listen to music. But Lance couldn't recall that his brother had ever been in trouble, except for the time when he beat up Clayton Miller.

His father's face disappeared, along with the kitchen on Fifth Avenue. His voice was gone too, and yet Lance had heard it so clearly. He felt shaken. The memory had surfaced without warning, and he had no control over it. It actually seemed a bit like a dream, even though that couldn't be right, since he was wide awake. Yet it seemed to have come from a part of his brain where dreams were born. And that was what had shaken him the most—more than the unpleasant memory, more than his father's voice. What was so shocking was that for a moment something inside Lance had been in touch with the land of dreams.

He started walking again. All around him the icicles clinked and clattered. It was nearly impossible to move without setting some of them in motion. He was still heading toward the Cross River and Baraga's Cross, since that was what they had agreed. But he knew full well that it no longer mattered. They weren't hunting anymore. He couldn't even fire his rifle. He just kept walking, or rather, pushing his way through the forest of icicles while the rain continued coming down, undiminished.

The woods ended, and he found himself near the highway. A slight slope would take him up to the guardrail. It wouldn't be hard to climb up since the ice hadn't yet settled on the tall grass covering the incline. He made his way up, grabbed hold of the guardrail, which was coated with a thick layer of ice, and peered over the edge.

Highway 61 gleamed as if it were a shimmery new type of road, cast from some sort of artificial material. The only sound Lance heard was the rain pouring down on the shiny, slick surface. He thought the world seemed deserted, as if all human beings had simultaneously departed. Everyone but him. On both sides of the road stood a forest of ice, as if even the trees had vanished, to be replaced by ice trees.

He maneuvered one leg over the guardrail and cautiously hauled the rest of his body over. It took great effort to stay upright. The slightest shift in weight might send him tumbling. But then he began moving away from the guardrail, taking tiny steps forward, without actually lifting his feet off the ice. When he reached the midpoint of the highway, he stopped. Even though he drove this road every single day, he wasn't exactly sure where he was. The ice made the woods unrecognizable. Many of the birches had started to lean over the road; a few were already bowed down under the weight of the ice. Over the next few hours quite a few trees were going to snap in half.

If Lance had stood here, motionless, under normal circumstances, he would have soon been hit by a vehicle coming around the curve. Maybe one of the semis that shuttled between Duluth and Thunder Bay in Canada. This was not a road where anyone should be standing in the middle of a downpour and expect to escape alive. But here he stood, unable to move at any great speed, and yet there was no danger. The only thing that was going to happen was that the rain would continue to fall. The ice would continue to thicken. Even more birch trees would start to lean over the road. The first trunk would snap with a dry, ripping sound. What was guaranteed *not* to happen was that some vehicle would show up. Or any people. All activity had ceased. This is what it would look like if everybody were dead, he thought. Everybody except for Lance Hansen. If that were the case, he would see the same thing he saw now. An empty road that would remain forever empty.

Or was this, instead, what it was like to be dead? When everyone else went on living, but he couldn't see them because he was on the other side of death's invisible wall? *Only the dead do not dream.* Maybe that was why he couldn't see anyone except for an Indian dressed in ragged old clothes. Because both he and the Indian were dead, and the dead could see only each other.

He squatted down, holding the completely ice-coated rifle in one hand as he ran the fingers of his other hand over the ice on the road. A couple of inches below his fingertips he could see the asphalt that he'd driven over only a short time ago. There it was, as if under glass, in full view but unreachable.

Just as unreachable as he was. Jimmy had tried to phone a dead man. That was why the boy had received no answer. There is no area code for the realm of the dead.

Lance sat down heavily on the ground. The slick Gore-Tex of his clothing created almost no friction on the icy road surface. And so he slowly started to slide. Up ahead the road sloped gently down toward a curve about a hundred yards away. After several yards his heavy body began to pick up momentum, and his speed noticeably increased. He grabbed the rifle and held it out in front of him, as if it were attached to invisible reins that, in turn, were attached to an invisible horse that was pulling him along the road. Inside the long block of ice he was holding, he could see the gun, like a dark shadow. He tried to stop the slide and get to his feet, but it was pointless; the road was much too slippery. All he could do was hold on to his ice rifle with hands that were aching with cold. The gun had cost him too much money to simply let it go. The invisible horse was going faster and faster through the rain. For a moment he thought with dread about what would happen if a car showed up, but then he remembered that wasn't going to happen. It *couldn't* happen. No one was capable of driving on this road right now. Lance was utterly alone on Highway 61.

He skidded and slowly began rotating to the left. His head, underneath the hood, was being steadily pelted by big raindrops, falling hard and fast. The backs of his hands too. His hands were crimson and almost completely numb. The icy forest, the gleaming road, the guardrail, the trees leaning so far forward that the icicles practically touched his head—everything rushed past in a blur, like the view seen from a carousel, going faster and faster, while he still held on to the shapeless rifle, as if the whole world might disappear if he lost his grip on the gun.

Turning counterclockwise, he slammed right into the ice-coated guardrail, careening like a runaway spinning top. Then he slid down the rest of the slope on his back, head first, with the rifle lying on his chest. He was afraid of running into something hard with his head, but a few moments later he came to a halt. He was lying in the middle of the road. Rain was pouring down onto his face. His left upper arm hurt from hitting the rail. It hurt so bad that at first he thought he might have broken his arm, but when he tried to move it, he was able to do so, even though he gasped in pain.

The birch trees, heavy with ice, leaned forward on either side of the road. They looked like big crystal chandeliers. He must be somewhere between the Temperance and the Cross Rivers, a stretch of road that he drove almost every day of the year, but right now he didn't recognize it at all. The ice had changed everything.

He sat up, dizzy after so much spinning around. With an effort he got to his feet and made his way over to the shoulder of the road. There was no guardrail here. He took another step and found himself on solid ground. A few more steps and he was once again standing among the birches. The icicles seemed dangerously heavy now that he was in among them. If any of them fell and struck his head, he would definitely be injured.

The best way to find out where he was in relation to the Cross River was probably to go down to the lake and look for Baraga's Cross, which was visible from quite a distance. Carefully he started forward under the bowed birch trees. As he moved, the icicles kept tapping against each other. Each icicle produced a different tone, depending on its size. Together they sounded as if someone were playing on a huge, untuned ice instrument.

He stopped to listen for anything that might indicate someone else was moving through this ice world along with him. He heard nothing but the rain striking the ice. As soon as he reached the parking lot, he'd find out whether his brother was still there or whether he'd driven off before the ice storm started. But first Lance wanted to go down to the lake to figure out how far it was to the parking area. He should be there soon. He just had to be careful not to tread on the slippery rocks.

Stooping a bit, Lance kept moving forward beneath

the overhanging ice, afraid that a big icicle might break off and hit his head. The vast, open space of the lake suddenly seemed extremely enticing, but he hadn't yet emerged from the woods. The forest went on and on. The feeling grew stronger that he was never going to reach the shore of the lake. He must have headed in the wrong direction, but how was that possible? Here? Between Highway 61 and Lake Superior? The strip of land between the water and the road was no more than a couple of hundred yards at the widest spot. How could he have missed the world's largest lake? And yet he seemed to have done exactly that, because the forest didn't end. Nor did it look any different.

The icicles formed a swaying latticework in every direction as they tapped against each other and against his ice-covered rifle. The cold, raw air gave him the feeling of being underwater, as if he were not moving among ice-laden birch trees but instead found himself deep inside an ocean that was in the process of freezing solid. An ocean or a lake. When he looked up he could no longer see the rainy gray sky. The trees were so coated with ice and so bowed down that they formed an impenetrable ceiling right above his head. It was getting a little harder to breathe, as if the weight of the ice were pressing on his lungs. What little light there was down here was being tossed back and forth between the swinging icicles. Fractured reflections of himself shimmered all around him.

Not a sound from outside. I can't sit here all night, but poking my head out the door would be the same as putting it on a chopping block if he's still alive. But there's no getting around it. If I stay here in this hut, I'll die of cold. I need to find Knut's boat shed. From there it's supposed to be a straight path up to their cabin. Knut and Nanette.

Fire in the hearth, porridge in my stomach. I get up onto my knees, holding the rifle in my hands. The ceiling is too low for me to stand up. It's now or never. Either I die or I arrive in America. With my left hand I cautiously move the birch bark aside. There he is, lying right in front of me in the moonlight. His hat has fallen off and is lying by itself a short distance away, but he's still wearing the scarf. He's on his back with his arms stretched out from his sides. His fur-clad boots are also pointing away. He looks like he's sleeping.

I crawl out and stand up, right next to his feet. Then I no longer feel the cold, even though I'm naked from the waist down. Nor do I notice the pain gnawing at me from inside. I stand there, barefoot in the snow, with a fire burning in my body. No one else can be allowed to see this. What I see right now is for me alone. The Indian is lying on the hard-packed snow. He's dead, and everything around me has turned so peaceful and quiet—inside me too. Except for a fire that's burning in my limbs. In my arms and legs. In my heart. It's so good to be alive in the middle of this forest, with this raging fire inside me. Now I can do anything. Should I just leave him lying here? But then someone might find him and see that he's been shot. The safest thing would be to get rid of him. I take a couple of steps forward and then stop next to his head. I look down at his face. At the black, longish hair sticking out from under the scarf. He's lying there in a big patch of moonlight. All around us are deep shadows. I can't see where the bullet hit him. Or any blood on the snow. Just as I think that one of his eyes seems to have opened slightly, his hand suddenly grabs my bare ankle. I let out a loud scream. His face is completely changed. He looks like a demon from the depths of hell. He yanks and pulls at my foot, trying to make me fall. I aim the rifle at his head and fire. Nothing but a hollow clack in the silence. I do it again, but the gun only clacks.

The Indian is shouting wildly at me. I throw myself at him. Straddle his chest with my naked loins. He's moving one hand, trying to find something. I know what he's looking for. I hold the gun with both hands and force the muzzle under his chin. Then I use my weight to crush his throat. I hear a gurgling sound. At first I feel something blazing hot, as if a cat has clamped its teeth into me. But then he pulls out the knife and strikes again. Another stab into my arm. I scream with pain. Force the rifle farther down. Hear something break inside him. His throat goes limp and soft like a dead kitten. His mouth is wide open. His eyes roll up. But I don't stop. I keep on killing him. It feels so good to kill. It feels so good not to be killed. It feels so good to arrive in America. I'm naked down below, and my manhood stands erect like a spear. I press harder and harder on that damned throat. A huge spasm passes through him. He shudders beneath me. The knife falls out of his hand. I'm injured, but feel only a heat in my arm where he stabbed me. I don't want to stop. This is the best feeling I've ever had.

LANCE TRIED to figure out where he was. He was sitting on the ground, and next to him lay the oblong block of ice with his rifle inside. It shouldn't be possible to get lost here, even under these conditions. It shouldn't be possible for *anyone*, much less for him. But he'd been walking and walking without reaching anyplace that looked familiar. All he'd seen the whole way was the same dense, ice-covered birch forest.

The upper part of his left arm was aching from hitting

the guardrail, and his whole body was probably black and blue after all the sliding around he'd done. Yet he would have preferred being back on the slippery road if he could just get out of this cold, raw stratum that formed the underbelly of the woods.

A surprising idea occurred to him. The more he thought about it, the more right it seemed. While he was sliding down the long slope, he'd spun around numerous times. When he finally came to a halt, he felt completely dizzy, and because of all the ice, both sides of the road had looked the same to him. Was it possible he'd entered the woods on the wrong side? He would have seen the same icy birch trees, no matter which side he chose.

If that was what happened, he had no idea where he was at the moment. There was no use trying to find the points of the compass if he couldn't catch a glimpse of the surrounding landscape. He might find his way back to the highway by sheer luck, but in theory he could also just keep on like this all the way to Canada. In reality, of course, he would die long before he ever got that far. Down here, under this roof of bowed, ice-laden birches, a partial twilight had already set in. He couldn't sit here for much longer. His only chance was to head in one direction and hope it would lead him out to the road, or to someplace else he recognized. But the problem was trying to keep moving in the same direction for any length of time when he had nothing to use to orient himself.

He stood up, feeling at once how the big, heavy icicles pressed against his back. Hunching over, he began moving forward. The strap of his rifle had become stiff, but he could still sling it over his shoulder. The big block of ice enclosing his rifle sent ripples of cold into his body. Because of all the ice touching his back and shoulder, he soon started feeling the effects of hypothermia. When he got out his cell phone, his fears were confirmed: there was no coverage. The tower on Leveaux Mountain must be down because of the ice.

For a while it felt like the terrain was rising steadily, and he wondered whether he was heading away from the lake and the road, toward the hills where he and Andy had been hunting earlier in the day. So he turned around and started off in the opposite direction, back toward where he'd come from. If he could just manage to stay on course, he should reach the highway eventually. But soon the terrain began rising again. He was about to turn around, when he realized how fruitless that would be. All he could do was keep going. If the ground was actually rising, that meant he was on his way north. And sooner or later he'd reach the belt of dense birch trees that extended from the shores of Lake Superior some distance up into the hills. In a more open type of forest he might have been able to orient himself. Right now it didn't seem likely that he could even hold a steady course northward. He was probably walking in circles. No doubt he was just imagining the slight incline.

In the back of his mind he was dreading the darkness, which was no more than an hour or so away. He did have a flashlight in his jacket pocket, but that wouldn't be much help as long as he could see only tree branches and ice in every direction. All day long he'd found it impossible to picture anything "after the hunt." It just didn't seem to exist for him. And now that was where he was headed, toward something that was simply cold and dark.

Soon he had to rest again. It was hard to walk stooped over, and besides, it felt good to put down his rifle, which was acting like a big cold-storage unit against his body. He lay down on the ground, stretching out full length. He lay there staring up at the chaos overhead. The slender birches were bowed under the weight of the ice, forming a tightly tangled web of branches visible through the shiny coating of ice. Hanging down from underneath everything were icicles of varying size, many of them so big that they might cause him serious injury. If he lay here long enough, one of them was bound to break off and fall. The biggest of them looked like they could skewer him. That was one way to die: skewered by ice.

His teeth had started to chatter. The muscles of his bulky torso were shivering. He knew this was his body's means of defense against the cold that was threatening to invade. If he didn't get indoors very soon, the cold would win. Yet he stayed where he was.

He tried to think of something pleasant, something that would make the time pass without too much anxiety. His thoughts stopped on three figures who were standing still, looking out across a darkened landscape, one big and two smaller figures. The moon was high in the sky, and below it, far in the distance, lay the lake, which faded off into space. Everything else was dark. The world consisted of the moon and Lake Superior. And those three people. Lance was looking at them from behind, but at the same time he remembered how it had felt to stand there, as one of them. What were they really doing there? His father had talked about something—that much he recalled. But about what? No, it was impossible to penetrate deeper into his memory, to grasp the words from that night at least thirty-five years ago.

Maybe he'd said something about their ancestors who had come to this lake from the island of Halsnøy, a place Lance had heard about all his life but never seen. As far back as he could remember, he'd heard about their ancestors who had settled at the base of Carlton Peak because the area reminded them of Tofte on Halsnøy. He didn't know whether that was true. Was that what his father had talked about as they stood there? *That's the stuff we're made of.*

Men who fell through the ice all alone and afterward survived a night in the woods with temperatures below freezing. These childish ideas about how it had all started. He'd run into them his whole life. The stories about what family surnames from Sweden and Norway actually meant, or why some great-great-grandfather had chosen that specific English name, which they all carried today. Rarely anything about the mundane reality behind it all—for instance, how their surnames had been hopelessly misspelled by the immigration authorities so that they became unrecognizable.

As he lay stretched out on the cold, raw forest floor beneath all those icy birch trees, Lance realized that the world his father had known had totally disintegrated. It simply no longer existed. What had once been the family's history had now been reduced to something so incomplete and chaotic that a life could never be built upon it. At least not the sort of life his parents had lived. The way things had turned out, Lance would have to stand on his own two feet without having an orderly and comprehensible past to support him. He would have to live with the incomplete, with the lack of logical coherence between all things, and accept that his own history was a dark abyss, a depth that could never be fathomed. He did not come from anything or anyone; he came from a big nothing.

Lance was no longer freezing. He had no idea how long he'd been lying here. By this point, he almost felt comfortable. Underneath this roof of ice, it was already dusk, but maybe dark was starting to fall outside the forest too. No one was going to come looking for him. Andy was not going to report him missing. By now he was probably back home watching TV with Tammy. An ordinary man who would continue to live a long life on the North Shore. Lance, on the other hand, was lying somewhere in the woods, noticing that he was starting to get tired, yet he did not enter the land of dreams. He felt only a numbness in his mind, as if he no longer had proper contact with himself.

I don't know where the lake is, he thought. He couldn't recall ever experiencing that before. The location of the lake was just as natural to him as the position of his own spine or feet, but right now he had no clue. Nor did he know where anything else was located.

A memory surfaced. They were sitting in his car outside the house where the Dupree family lived. Mary's room was on the second floor of her parents' home. Lance used to drive her home in the evening. This was while they were still just dating. Suddenly Mary said, *"We call the moon in July Ode'imini-giizis. The strawberry moon. Isn't that lovely, Lance?"* And the strawberry moon had shone big and golden above the treetops.

He could no longer imagine any way forward. He had reached the end of the road. Lance thought about Jimmy. For some reason he pictured his son sitting in the bow of a canoe that was gliding through the water. His face was pale. No one was paddling the canoe; it was moving all on its own, swiftly carrying his son away from Lance. Finally he could see only the boy's face, like a small pale patch off in the distance. Just as his face was about to disappear, Jimmy shouted something. He was too far away for Lance to make out what he said; it sounded like little more than a bird cheeping. Then the great expanse of water was once more empty and still.

Now he heard it again. His son was calling him from beyond the horizon. Lance opened his eyes and looked up at the threatening icicles above. There it was again, a voice far away. But this was real. Someone was shouting! He tried to sit up, but his body refused to obey. It sounded like someone was calling his name. He tried again, and this time he managed to sit. His head ached, and his teeth were chattering.

Then he heard it loud and clear, right nearby. "Lance!" He tried to answer, but he'd lost his voice. A hoarse whisper way down in his throat was all he could muster. He tried again, but he was incapable of uttering any sound that would carry farther than a couple of yards.

He got up on his knees and grabbed his ice-coated gun. Then he forced himself to stand, at the same time slinging the strap of the rifle over his shoulder. The touch of the ice on his body almost sent him toppling to the ground again, but he couldn't lie down now. Somebody was here. He took a few hesitant steps, squeezing in between the birch trees. The icicles clinked against each other. No more shouts. That wasn't so strange, since he hadn't answered. Besides, it was just a voice he'd heard inside his own head. That was what he now realized, because he knew who the voice belonged to. His father, Oscar. He was the one who had called his name. And Oscar Hansen was with the dead.

Even so, Lance started walking in the direction he thought he'd heard the voice coming from. Soon he noticed a sound he hadn't heard in a long while. Raindrops striking his hood. Up ahead was the huge, gray surface of Lake Superior.

The sight of the lake should have made him feel relieved, maybe even happy. Because now he knew where he was—except for the fact that the lake couldn't possibly be here or he would have found it long ago. So he felt as if he'd come upon a different lake. One that looked exactly like the one he knew, with the same expanse of rocks and the same birch forest; yet it was not the same. As if Lake Superior had a twin that he only now had discovered. One that had been waiting for him in a completely different place. And now he had finally reached that other place.

I can't die now, not when I've finally managed to get my frozen underwear and homespun pants back on. It feels like putting on the lake, my clothes are so cold. I drop his arms and lean against the thick trunk of a pine tree. My injured arm is burning hot and throbbing. In front of me flows the black river. All I hear is a faint gurgling sound. The rocks sticking up from the water wear tall hats of snow. In the open space, where the river runs into the lake, the moonlight glitters on the water.

"Thou shalt not kill. That is: We shall fear and love God so that we do no harm to our neighbor nor injury to his body, but rather help him and lend him aid in all jeopardy and peril." Is he my neighbor, the man lying there on the snow? I no longer remember why I did it, only that I had to. For me to live, he had to die. I kneel down and lower my hand to the dead face. Let it hover there, an inch above the stranger's dark skin. Then I touch him. Feel the beaked nose. Place my hand on his forehead. If I can just get him out to the open water and under the edge of the ice, they might never find him. The cross is casting a long shadow. Maybe Knut put up the cross to keep the heathens away. If so, his cabin can't be far off.

I start dragging the Indian across the snow again, leaving a long, wide trail of blood. If anyone comes here, they'll know what happened. I have to pray to God that snow will fall before any folks arrive. But do I have a right to pray to God for help after I've taken a human life? He must have been a wild savage. Someone who worshipped idols. If so, I don't know whether it counts as murder. I let go of him again. Everything starts spinning before my eyes. The blood on the snow is from both of us. Now the lake rises up like a wall. Stars are falling down on me and inside me. They're hot as they fall through my chest and stomach. I fall as light as a feather from a very tiny bird. But then I see that I've already landed and am lying on the snow. My face hurts. I must have scraped my cheek when I fell. I'm not going to make it. I see that now. I am never going to reach Knut and Nanette. Everything was going so well. I didn't encounter any particular hardships getting this far, but tonight everything has gone wrong. The last night. Now I'm lying here, probably not very far from their home, and I can no longer get up. The dead Indian is lying next to me. He smells terrible. Is it from the animals he has flayed? There were rows of pelts hanging outside his hut. Or is this just the way savages smell? Now I notice that he smells of shit too. He has shit his pants. I manage to wriggle out my good arm, which I landed on when I fell, and I place my hand on his chest. It takes a moment, but then I feel a faint warmth under my hand. That's what I thought. He hasn't gone cold yet. There's nothing to be scared of, Thormod. The dead can't hurt you.

Cautiously I crawl closer to him. I lie there, feeling a warmth start to seep over me. It takes awhile, because there's not much warmth left, but I want what little there is. All I need is a little warmth. I try to climb on top of him, but it's hard to do because of the pain. I try again, and I manage to place one leg over his leg and haul myself halfway up onto him. But his clothes are almost as cold as my own. I stick one hand under his shirt and touch his soft belly. Instantly I feel sticky blood and warmth on the palm of my hand. The warmth that I want. I take out my knife and start cutting off his clothes. Underneath he's wearing another thick woolen shirt. I cut through everything, from his neck to his waist, and move the clothing aside so his naked skin is bare underneath me. The hole in his stomach is round and black. After much effort I manage to take off my jacket. Then I roll my shirt up under my arms as best I can. May God forgive me for this sin, but if I don't do it, I will die.

While something gnaws and stabs deep inside me, like bone against bone, I climb on top of the Indian and press my naked skin against his. I feel his blood on my stomach. The warmth starts flowing into me. I spread out my shirt behind me so that my back is not completely exposed to the cold air. I tilt my head back as far as possible so that my face won't touch his, but that soon grows tiring. I simply have to lay my head down. Rest against him. And that's what I do. I lay my head on his shoulder, cheek to cheek, my nose pressed against the scarf he's wearing on his head.

Something strange happens as I lie here like this. I don't know what it is, but it feels like a fall, like I'm falling into him. There's a rushing sound all around me. The whole time I'm falling into the other body that's lying here, his skin pressed against my skin. I cling to him as I fall into him, or into something that was him only a short time ago, but it's no longer anyone. The remains of something. I notice that he's no longer inside his body, which now belongs equally to me, since I was the one who killed him. I crushed his Adam's apple and his throat. Sat there naked from the waist down, with my naked loins straddling his chest, my manhood erect when I killed him. Now I'm falling into the empty space that is left of him. As I lie here, falling, I can also see myself from far overhead, as if I were once again up there among the stars. I see myself lying on top of a dead man. All around us are the big spruce trees and a vast lake.

From up here I can see how far I am from home. On one side of the ocean I see Halsnøy, so green and beautiful, with the islands of Fjelberg and Borgundøy very close. On the other side is the huge land that I've been traveling deeper and deeper into, past towns that didn't look like anything I've ever seen before, not even in my dreams, with trains moving along the biggest rivers and over the longest bridges, horse-drawn carts passing between trees so enormous that you'd think you were in the Old Testament. Farther and farther away from Halsnøy. Until I arrived here. I can see myself far below, near the big lake, only an hour or two from where my uncle lives. I see his log cabin in the woods. Smoke is coming from the chimney. But that is a place I will never reach. I'm just lying there, clinging to the man I killed. Sucking the warmth out of him. A short distance away from us the cross is casting a shadow on the snow. And the rushing sound of my fall continues into the dead man. Soon I will be completely inside him. Trapped inside the other body. Then I will get up and go, and my own body will be left there in place of his.

Soon I'll be able to walk through the woods as an Indian. But then I can't knock on the door of the cabin where Knut and Nanette live. They would never let a savage inside. I will have to wander around alone in the forest and feel his shit in my pants. Never be warm again, never be able to eat. I lift my face and see that he is standing next to us. He's lying underneath me and he's standing next to us. But he doesn't look fully alive as he stands there. More like something from a dream. Or is that me? Have I already stood up inside his body? Am I the one standing there? He doesn't look angry. Instead, he looks like he's about to cry. Then he slowly starts walking toward the woods. I'm afraid that might be me walking away, and I don't want to lose myself. But I watch as he disappears over there among the spruce trees.

I open my eyes and look around. It's so cold. Did I fall asleep? Underneath me is the dead Indian. I no longer feel warm. I try to get up, but my body is so stiff I can hardly move. I'll just have to stay here and die. The cross is already here, after all. I'm about to give up, but then I remember seeing the world from high overhead. And when I did that, I saw the cabin where Knut and Nanette live. With smoke coming from the chimney. And it's not very far away. I think I can make it. But first I have to get to my feet. I force my frozen body to move and scream with pain in that white, empty night. Finally I manage to stand up. My legs don't feel like they belong to me anymore; I can hardly feel them. My body is made of glass. That's how it feels, as if I'm made of the most delicate glass.

I turn to look toward the cross and the strip of open water. So close, and yet so far away. I'm going to die now, I tell myself. Either that, or I take the Indian and drag him farther. Then I lean down and grab his arms. It feels like I'm leaning out of myself, that my body remains standing upright, while my will or my mind leans down to grab the Indian. Only after I straighten up and stand there, holding his wrists, do I return to myself. It was as if my immortal soul had leaned out of me. I have no strength left, but something else takes over. There is someone else inside me, someone who drags both me and the Indian. Slowly I approach the cross. Maybe I'm sleepwalking. It keeps getting easier. Now my legs are hovering above the snow. I'm gliding through the air. No,

*I'm lying on my back and looking up at the cross above me.
In this place it's probably not possible to find anything more
Christian than that. The Indian went into the woods. I remember that. Or was I the one who stood up inside his body
and left? One of us left. That much I know. One of us is out
there somewhere.*

THERE WAS NO SIGN OF LIFE. Not so much as a duck on
the water. No Taconite Harbor to the southwest, with white
smoke coming from the electrical power plant. No sounds
from the road. The rain was coming down harder, the drops
pelting his Gore-Tex clothing. Dusk had started seeping
into the vast space over the lake. Soon it would be completely dark, and Lance had nothing to help him except the
flashlight in his jacket pocket. It would be life-threatening
to walk along the rocks, with only the beam from the small
bulb. And the flashlight would be of little use inside the
woods, where he'd be able to see only a couple of yards
ahead of him.

He'd heard a voice . . . If not for the voice, he would have
kept lying on the ground someplace in the birch forest, and
that was where he would have stayed. The voice had saved
him. But was it a real voice? Or was it just something he'd
heard inside his own head?

He decided not to let the lake out of his sight. The last
thing he wanted was to end up in the labyrinth of ice-coated
birches again. So he kept to the narrow border area between
the woods and those treacherous rocks. Here the ground
was mostly heath and grass, also covered with ice, but not
in big slippery patches, so it was easier to walk.

He soon came to a place where the gently sloping rocks
gave way to an abrupt cliff nearly ten feet high, with the
woods stretching all the way to the base of the rock preci-

pice. He wouldn't be able to climb along the cliff. To continue on he would have to go back into the woods, just for a short distance, but he wasn't confident he'd be able to find his way back to the lake if he did.

The branches of the bowed trees were so intertwined and so laden with icicles that the forest seemed almost impenetrable. Yet he had no choice. This was not a place where he could stay. He looked around. He saw only the gray surface of the water and ice. Darkness was quickly falling.

It was just a slight twitch of a few branches. Something was moving at the edge of the woods, maybe a hundred yards away. He wasn't sure what he'd seen. It could have been a deer, but it could also have been a person.

Lance went over to the wall of ice-coated birch trees. He was still shivering from the cold, and his head ached, yet he had no choice but to force his way through the tangle of branches and leaning tree trunks. As soon as he did, the forest closed behind him and everything looked exactly the same. For a moment he felt panic spreading through him. Then he regained control. He knew the lake was right behind him. Now all he had to do was to veer left in order to come out on the other side of the cliff that had blocked his path along the water. He kept on going, toiling to shove aside the big, dangling icicles, which clinked against each other. The sound of ice striking ice accompanied him as he made his way forward. After a while doubt again crept over him. He should have emerged from the woods by now. Hadn't he kept far enough to the left? Or had he veered too much, so that he was walking in circles? He couldn't figure out what had happened. All he could do was keep going, without really believing he would get anywhere. He was starting to think he was back in the same confusing labyrinth where he'd been only a short while ago.

Suddenly he came to a clearing. He could make out the

contours of a vehicle beneath a thick layer of ice. On the other side of the clearing there seemed to be a road or a path. A sort of tunnel beneath the bowed and broken birch trees. He realized he was looking at the parking area near Baraga's Cross. He almost didn't recognize it. That must be Andy's Chevy Blazer under all that ice. He took a step forward. His feet instantly slipped out from under him and he crashed to the ground, landing hard on his left elbow. He sat there, moaning with the pain. His rifle lay next to him; the ice coating had cracked when it struck the ground. Now the gun lay there as if brand new, pulled right from the mold. He picked up the rifle and inspected it. There was still a little ice here and there, but it would no longer act like a cold storage unit against his body. And the scope seemed to be intact.

He got up and cautiously made his way over to the Chevy. He couldn't see in the windows. Maybe Andy's sitting inside, he thought. No, why would he be doing that? But he obviously hadn't gone home, so he must be around here somewhere. Lance thought about the branches he'd noticed moving a while ago. Maybe that was Andy. If so, he had to be nearby. But did he realize Lance was standing next to his vehicle?

Lance now reacted quickly. He crossed the mirror-smooth parking lot as fast as he dared and forced himself to go back into the woods. If he could manage to walk straight ahead, he should soon reach the Cross River right above Baraga's Cross. Andy wouldn't be expecting him to come from that direction.

After a few minutes he saw the river through the tree branches, and he was soon standing on the bank. Broken, icy trees hung out over the river on both sides. The rocks sticking up out of the water had strange domes of ice on top. Something moved at the very edge of his peripheral vision.

He turned at once and caught sight of a man disappearing into the woods. This time he wouldn't get away.

Lance started walking along the river, but he'd gone no more than a few yards when the man came back out of the woods a little farther down, near the cross. Lance took a step back and stood partially hidden behind a bowed birch. Then he raised his rifle, which was now released from its heavy burden of ice, and placed the buttstock against his shoulder. Through the scope he could see the man clearly.

It was Andy.

Lance stood as still as if he were stalking a deer. His brother was about twenty yards away from Baraga's Cross, just about where the expanse of rocks began. It took an effort to stand there so long with the rifle in firing position, and Lance could feel the strain in his arms and shoulders. But many times he'd stood even longer without starting to shake. He had Andy in the crosshairs. Right between the shoulder blades. Soon it would be impossible to see him at all in the rapidly growing darkness. A triumphant feeling surged inside Lance. He tried to release the safety with his thumb, but it refused to budge. There must still be some ice in the mechanism. He tried again, but he couldn't flick off the safety. Annoyed, he pressed on the trigger, but of course it wouldn't move as long as the safety was on. He squeezed harder. The whole time he kept the crosshairs fixed on the same spot between his brother's shoulders. Nothing happened. The telescopic scope was a dark tunnel, in which nothing existed except for him and Andy. Lance's eye at one end, his brother's back at the other. And beyond his brother stood Baraga's Cross, on the verge of being erased by the darkness settling over the lake. He could just make out the long, rough icicles hanging from the two arms of the cross.

Andy turned around and looked straight at him. Through the powerful lenses Lance saw something click into place on his brother's face. Then Andy set off running toward the protective wall of the ice-covered forest. The last Lance saw of him, he had pulled his rifle from his shoulder and was running with the gun in his hand, like a soldier in battle. A couple of icy branches swayed slightly at the spot where he disappeared into the woods. Then once again everything was still.

The situation had been turned on its head. Now it was Lance who stood exposed, and he felt drained of all strength. He'd lain too long on the ground, and the cold had penetrated so deeply into him that it couldn't be driven out. It had settled on the inside of his skull. But the cold was no longer the greatest threat. Nor was the darkness, which was fast becoming impermeable among the trees. It was his brother he feared. He was somewhere very close. Lance's rifle was unusable, but Andy didn't know that. He had turned around and looked up along the river, and there he had seen Lance taking aim at him.

As Lance made his way through the dense, icy underbrush, it got so dark he could hardly see a thing anymore. He could barely even make out his hand when he waved it a foot or so in front of his face. And he couldn't use the flashlight as long as Andy was searching for him. He had no idea where his brother was in relation to his own position; he heard only the rustle of his own Gore-Tex clothing and the icicles striking each other as he shoved them aside. Andy was a thin and agile man, with a unique ability to sneak up on his prey. He would have no difficulty coming upon Lance unawares in the dense woods. With all the ice covering the trees, the sound of a shot wouldn't travel far, and besides it was unlikely anyone was around to hear it.

He felt like he was inside a cold, dark sack in which there was no longer any air to breathe. Lance was about to give up and lie down on the ground when he glimpsed something up ahead. He took a few more steps and saw that he had reached the edge of the parking area. Here a glimmer of light still remained. No more than a trace of gray in the darkness, but enough for him to discern the outline of the frost-covered vehicle. If he followed the perimeter of the parking lot to the left, he would soon reach Baraga Cross Road, which led up to Highway 61. He had no idea what good that would do, yet it felt like his only option. Maybe it was simply because the road connected all the places that were important to him in this small world of his—from Duluth to Grand Portage.

He started walking along the edge of the parking lot. Twice he slipped and fell, but finally he saw an open area under the broken trees. That had to be Baraga Cross Road. He stooped and went in. Now it was obvious he'd found the road, but he had a hard time making his way along the ice-covered asphalt, and he fell again and again. Finally he was so exhausted he couldn't get himself to stand up anymore; he simply rolled over onto his back. His rifle lay across his chest. He gripped it with both hands, keeping his right index finger curled around the frozen trigger.

Then he clearly heard the sound of ice against ice very close by. Someone was coming, and it couldn't be anyone but Andy. Would his brother find him in the dark? Lance's only chance was to lie still as a mouse and then maybe Andy would walk right past. Or trip over him. There was no doubt that he was here. Lance could even hear him breathing. But all the ice was distorting the sound so much that he couldn't tell where it was coming from. It seemed to be coming from every direction at once. All he could do was lie still in the dark and wait.

He happened to think about the white cat. How it had lain there in the beam from his flashlight, unable to move. He took a tighter grip on his rifle, pressed his finger harder on the trigger. All around him in the dark he heard his brother breathing—it was a sound that had always been present, although Lance hadn't given it much thought. In the darkness of the room they'd shared as kids, before they each had their own room. Next to him in the backseat of the car; sometimes against his shoulder, with drool seeping out of Andy's mouth. And on a September day in the school yard, with a baseball bat in his hand and an expression that was the loneliest sight Lance had ever seen. Always that same breathing.

And now he could hear it coming from every direction in the dark all around him. He tightened his grip on the rifle. At the same time there was something restrained about it, as if his brother were doing everything he could not to be heard. He was keeping his breaths as short and subdued as Lance was doing. And yet his breathing resounded inside Lance's head.

Andy had seen him standing there, taking aim. Now Lance was the one being hunted. A sense of lightness was growing inside him. It began to swell, and the sound of Andy's breathing swelled with it, getting steadily louder as it spread, as if it might soon be the only thing that existed.

That was when something occurred to Lance: *Could it be my own breathing I'm hearing?* He held his breath and listened. A moment later Andy's breathing stopped too. Or was it his own that had stopped? He released it with a slight whistle, scared his brother would hear. Then he listened. Yes, it was still there. The same breathing. Again Lance held his breath. The same thing happened. A few seconds passed, and then the other breathing stopped too. And when he allowed himself to breathe once again, he heard the other person start breathing too. If it was Andy he heard, it must mean that Andy could also hear him. Was his brother standing right next to him in the dark, hearing the very same thing he heard? Was he also surrounded by his brother's breathing? Maybe that was why nothing happened—because Andy didn't know where Lance was in the darkness all around them. Maybe he was standing there, waiting for Lance to give away his location.

He held his breath again. This time the other person also stopped breathing a couple of seconds later.

Suddenly Andy's voice pierced the silence.

"Lance?" the voice whispered.

He was just about to answer, but realized at the last moment that it was a trap. If he replied, he would reveal where he was. He didn't even dare breathe, just held his rifle in a tight grip.

"You're a dead man, Lance," Andy whispered.

He felt the trigger give way, but he couldn't stop it. The bang struck his eardrums like a hammer against an anvil. The darkness exploded in yellow and orange. A brief cry sounded right near him. Then he heard the body topple over with icicles clinking all around.

Above us are two birch branches lashed together with some sort of rope. If only I can get to my feet, I can tumble him into the open strip of water. But my body refuses. I try. I can hear myself screaming and carrying on. It's like hearing something from far away. As if I'm standing somewhere in the woods, listening to a madman screaming and carrying on near the cross. I'm standing over there behind a tree. I must have been the one who went into the forest. I got up inside the other body and left. Now I'm an Indian in the woods. No, that's crazy! I killed him. He's lying right here. I'm glad I remembered to hide the ax. If I hadn't done that, they probably would have found it. Because someday someone will come here. And they would have seen that it's a white man's ax. But I hid it under a spruce tree. It will probably stay there for a long time before anyone finds it. But you never know, so I can't feel completely safe. Never again completely safe. If I don't get up soon, I'll die. The cabin where Knut lives. It's there in the woods, not far away, with smoke coming from the chimney. If only I can get there, no one can stop me. Then I will finally have arrived in America—someone who has killed a man in order to get there.

With a hollow shriek in a voice I don't recognize, I get up on my knees. Out there is the treacherous ice that I tried to walk across. I can see the hole where I fell in. Beyond the ice lies the lake, black and glittering. I'm going to haul up all the big fish that live down there. Every single one. Fragile as glass, I get to my feet and stand up straight. Lean one hand on the cross. Look out at the lake. The other hand is wet with blood. My own, I think. A ripping sensation inside me when I breathe. My mouth is swollen with cuts and blood left when my lips froze to the crusted snow. They've been left behind somewhere in the woods, those lips that I used to talk with back home. What kind of place is this, anyway? A cross on a desolate spit of land. Maybe they had to chase the heathens away when they first came here. And that's why they put up the cross, to frighten them. I press my forehead to the cross and think about God and Jesus. And about the pastor who confirmed me. I pray to all three, asking forgiveness for what I've done. Then I go over to the dead man, lean down, and with a strength I didn't know I had, I drag him the last short distance down to the open strip of water. There I drop him, so that he's lying at the very edge. All it will take is a small push and he'll slide out. But is the current strong enough to carry him out into the water and under the edge of the ice? There's only one way to find out. I set my foot on him, about to send him off, but it seems inhuman to do it like that. To just send him off, out into the dark, cold water. But I've already killed him, so why can't I get rid of his body? He's nothing more than a piece of meat. But he's lying there with that broad, dark face of his turned toward me. His eyes half open. That big, beaked nose. Open mouth. Black hair, a little longer than mine, is sticking out from under the scarf.

Only now do I wonder who he is. He must have family, just as I do. People who will miss him. And he must have a name, which they will say when they talk about the fact that he has disappeared. The name that his mother must have used to call him when he was a boy, just as my mother called for me. But now they can shout all they like. I set my foot against his hip and push, but his body is heavy and I am so weak. At first he doesn't budge. Then I manage to move the middle of his body a few inches. I try again, but I have no more strength left and can't even stay on my feet. I sit down beside him. He's lying at the very edge. One arm is hanging down toward the water. It wouldn't take much to send him into the current, but even that is too much for me. As I sit there like that, he slips out all on his own. One arm sketches an arc toward the black river, then his body hits the water with a loud splash. Slowly he drifts toward the edge of the ice. I fought him like a lion, and won. He's the one lying there with his face in the cold, dark water while I sit here, alive, and watch. His head rams into the ice. His body blocks the current like a log. The water ripples around him. I hear a faint gurgling sound. The current is stronger than I thought. Now the body turns until it's stretched out

VIDAR SUNDSTØL is the acclaimed Norwegian author of seven novels, including the Minnesota Trilogy, written after he and his wife lived for two years on the North Shore of Lake Superior. *The Land of Dreams* (Minnesota, 2013), the first novel in the trilogy, was awarded the Riverton Prize for best Norwegian crime novel of 2008 and was nominated for the Glass Key for best Scandinavian crime novel of the year. *The Land of Dreams* was ranked by *Dagbladet* as one of the top twenty-five Norwegian crime novels, and the Minnesota Trilogy has been translated into seven languages.

TIINA NUNNALLY is an award-winning translator of Danish, Norwegian, and Swedish literature. Her many translations include Sigrid Undset's first book, *Marta Oulie: A Novel of Betrayal* (Minnesota, 2014). Her translation of Undset's *Kristin Lavransdatter III: The Cross* won the PEN/Book-of-the-Month Club Translation Prize. She was appointed Knight of the Royal Norwegian Order of Merit for her efforts on behalf of Norwegian literature in the United States.